Bolan waited for the signal from Grimaldi, then leaped into the storm.

The Cessna's slipstream carried Bolan backward, his arms and legs splayed, then the plane was gone and gale-force winds attacked him like a sentient enemy. His goggles frosted over almost instantly.

From thirteen thousand feet, Bolan had about two minutes until he'd hit the ground below. Ninety seconds before he reached four thousand feet and had to deploy his main chute. If he dropped any lower without pulling the ripcord, the reserve chute would deploy automatically in time to save his life.

In theory.

At the moment, though, Bolan was spinning like a dreidel in a cyclone, blinded by the snow and frost on his goggles, hoping he could catch a glimpse of the altimeter attached to his left glove. Without it, he'd have to rely on counting seconds in his head. A miscalculation, and he'd be handing his life over to the emergency chute's activation device, hoping it would prevent him from plummeting to certain death in the Sierras.

If he didn't survive this jump, it could mean a massacre. A dozen lives, maybe two or three times more, depended on him without those people knowing it. If he arrived in time, unbroken, and could circumvent the coming siege…

A burst of wind spun Bolan counterclockwise, flipped him over on his back, th[...]
facing the jagged peaks [...]
the worst of it and reach[...]

Breathing through clenc[...]
reached up to grasp the [...]

MACK BOLAN ®
The Executioner

THE EXECUTIONER

DON PENDLETON'S

DARK SAVIOR

A GOLD EAGLE BOOK FROM

WORLDWIDE.

TORONTO • NEW YORK • LONDON
AMSTERDAM • PARIS • SYDNEY • HAMBURG
STOCKHOLM • ATHENS • TOKYO • MILAN
MADRID • WARSAW • BUDAPEST • AUCKLAND

For Special Deputy US Marshal Frank E. McKnight
End of Watch: May 29, 2014

First edition November 2015

ISBN-13: 978-0-373-64444-5

Special thanks and acknowledgment to
Mike Newton for his contribution to this work.

Dark Savior

Recycling programs
for this product may
not exist in your area.

Printed in U.S.A.

There is a heroism in crime as well as in virtue.
—William Hazlitt

If the law must be bent in the service of justice, so be it. I do what's necessary to defend innocent lives. End of story.
—Mack Bolan

THE
MACK BOLAN
LEGEND

Nothing less than a war could have fashioned the destiny of the man called Mack Bolan. Bolan earned the Executioner title in the jungle hell of Vietnam.

But this soldier also wore another name—Sergeant Mercy. He was so tagged because of the compassion he showed to wounded comrades-in-arms and Vietnamese civilians.

Mack Bolan's second tour of duty ended prematurely when he was given emergency leave to return home and bury his family, victims of the Mob. Then he declared a one-man war against the Mafia.

He confronted the Families head-on from coast to coast, and soon a hope of victory began to appear. But Bolan had broken society's every rule. That same society started gunning for this elusive warrior—to no avail.

So Bolan was offered amnesty to work within the system against terrorism. This time, as an employee of Uncle Sam, Bolan became Colonel John Phoenix. With a command center at Stony Man Farm in Virginia, he and his new allies—Able Team and Phoenix Force—waged relentless war on a new adversary: the KGB.

But when his one true love, April Rose, died at the hands of the Soviet terror machine, Bolan severed all ties with Establishment authority.

Now, after a lengthy lone-wolf struggle and much soul-searching, the Executioner has agreed to enter an "arm's-length" alliance with his government once more, reserving the right to pursue personal missions in his Everlasting War.

Prologue

Las Cruces, New Mexico

"It's hot," Rob Walker said.

"You say that every day. New Mexico," Greg Kilhane replied. "It's *always* hot."

"Hotter today than usual." Walker used a handkerchief to blot his sweaty face.

Kilhane, who never seemed to sweat, drew on his cigarette and shook his head. "Go back inside, then. I can handle this alone."

The two of them were standing on the patio so Kilhane could smoke. No smoking in the safe house under the established guidelines. Nearly dusk, and it was still too hot for Walker's liking, but he'd come out anyway and left their third man with their subject.

"Don't mind me," said Walker. "Just keep poisoning yourself."

Bitching was part of witness duty with the U.S. Marshals Service. Guarding rats was tedious, dead time, when they could just as well have been out serving warrants, busting fugitives, transporting prisoners from jail to court or court to prison. Anything was better, more exciting, than babysitting squealers in the Witness Security Program.

"Only two more days," Kilhane said.

Until their witnesses testified, that was. Which meant they'd all be flying out the day after tomorrow, headed back to New York City and the high life, handing off their pigeon to the Special Operations Group for coverage until he testified against whomever he'd decided to betray in exchange for a new name, new life, new whatever.

Walker didn't know the details of the case, except that it was "big," according to the supervisory deputy who'd handed them the assignment. "Big as in bad guys with billions," he'd said, a real wisecracker.

That raised the threat level and meant they had two AR-15 rifles and a shotgun at the safe house, in addition to their standard-issue .40-caliber Glocks. There were vests in the house, one for each marshal and a spare for the rat, but Walker hadn't tried his on and wouldn't bother with it till they headed for the airport, day after tomorrow.

Easy duty, sure, but boring. And hot today, as usual, even at sundown.

"Done yet?" he asked Kilhane.

"Are you the nicotine police?"

"Forget it."

Kilhane stubbed his butt into a three-foot-tall ceramic ashtray filled with sand, and sighed smoke. "Yeah, I'm done. Let's make sure Marshal Marshall hasn't lost the subject."

Walker laughed at that, the way he always did, on reflex. Ethan Marshall was their third team member, "Marshal Marshall" to the others like Kilhane, who couldn't let it go. Sometimes Walker wondered if he'd gotten out of high school, after all. Still hanging out with jocks and trading silly puns, except the stakes were higher. If he dropped the ball on this job, it could cost him his life.

"THEY'RE GOING BACK INSIDE," Killer Combs said. "Over."

A second later Spike O'Connor's voice came back to him, the walkie-talkie giving it a tinny echo. "Copy that. Let's do it."

"Roger that," Combs responded.

His mama hadn't named him Killer. She had called him Cleveland, of all things, and that had drawn the schoolyard bullies like a magnet pulls iron filings from the dirt, until Combs taught them that he didn't swallow any shit. "Killer" came from buddies in United States Marine Corps Force Reconnaissance, two tours of duty in Iraq, one in Afghanistan. Combs might've still been in the Corps, maybe a master sergeant by now, if slotting Afghans and Iraqis hadn't turned him on so much. If only he'd restrained himself a bit that day, outside of Lashkar Gah.

To hell with it, he thought, and moved out toward their target. It felt strange, working inside the States and with a dozen guys involved, but who was he to question clients with that kind of cash to throw around? They wanted certainty, an ironclad guarantee that no one in the house would ever bother them again, with cell phone snaps to prove the job was done.

Quirky, but what the hell.

"You heard the man," he told Cohen and Hitchener. "Let's roll."

"WHERE'S WALKER?" KILHANE asked Ethan Marshall.

"In the crapper."

"Jeez. How long has he been in there, anyway?"

Marshall considered that, checking the TV against his watch, the six o'clock news winding down into sports and weather. "Twenty minutes, give or take," he said.

That put a frown on Kilhane's face. "I'm gonna check on him and—"

The second part of his sentence was cut off as the doorbell rang. Walker emerged from the bathroom.

"Who's that?" Walker asked.

"How the hell should I know?" Marshall countered. "Jehovah's Witnesses? Or maybe Girl Scouts pushing cookies." He rose from the sofa and unholstered his Glock.

"Check it," Kilhane said to Walker. And to Marshall, "Back him up. I'm going for the subject."

"Right," Walker replied, the three of them all business now.

"Up and at it," Kilhane ordered. "This is not a drill."

COLIN HUME WAS dressed up in a brown UPS uniform, the van they'd stolen for the evening behind him, idling at the curb. His parcel was a cardboard box large enough to hold a Bizon submachine gun with fifty-three 9 mm Parabellum packed into its helical magazine, ready to rip. Hume had cut out the back of the box, and now he slid his right hand inside to clutch the Bizon's pistol grip. A clipboard balanced up on top helped his cover.

He was on the verge of trying the doorbell again when a voice from inside asked, "Who is it?"

Hume smiled at the peephole in the door, its blocking shadow proof that someone was already eyeing him. "Parcel delivery," he answered, adding a mush-mouth garble for a name.

"What's that?" the man behind the door demanded.

Hume spat out another mess of jumbled syllables, his index finger on the Bizon's trigger, that part of the weapon borrowed from larger rifles designed by its creator, the great Viktor Kalashnikov.

Some men were giants in their field. Others, like Colin Hume, stood on their shoulders for a better shot at whoever was marked for death today.

"Hang on," the guy behind the door said now, clearly disgruntled, maybe wondering if he should get his ears checked. Hume kept smiling as a dead bolt clacked, and then the door began to open.

Easy does it...

Hume waited until he had a clear view of the doorman, checked him with a glance to see if he was wearing Kevlar underneath his wilted dress shirt, then fired a six-round burst into the stranger's chest. The Parabellum rounds slammed the guy backward as he spouted crimson from a tidy group of holes above his heart, and Hume pushed through the doorway into a small sitting room.

The second marshal waited for him there, as Hume had expected, wielding his Glock but firing just a beat too slow, still not quite believing that he'd seen his partner killed before his eyes.

Hume dropped to one knee, ditched the smoking box and gave the second guard two short precision bursts. The first one opened up his belly before the second caught him doubling over, tattooing his startled face.

Two down, but there were three guards on the target. Hume went looking for the third. The back door opened with a bang, three of his team members moving in to help him sweep the place. Two more were close behind Hume, bulling through the front door he'd left open, which left six outside in various positions, covering the action from a distance, watching for police.

O'Connor, the leader of the operation, began barking orders, and the men fanned out to check the other rooms. Each of them had the floor plan memorized: kitchen and a smallish dining room to the right, four bedrooms, one en suite, and a separate bathroom all off to Hume's left, down a hallway. In front of him, glass sliding doors faced the desert and a backyard somebody had stripped of grass, replacing it with rocks and cacti.

As Hume started for the hallway, Mueller and Ornelas jogged past him, not wanting to let him hog the fun. He didn't hurry, knowing that the third watchdog would come to them after he'd heard the racket in the living room.

Safe house, my ass, Hume thought, smiling.

Even if number three were on the phone right now, making a panic call, the reinforcements wouldn't come in time to save him or the target he was guarding. They were out of time, beyond salvation now.

As if on cue, the third marshal showed himself, clearing the hallway in a rush, an AR-15 at his shoulder. He was clearly stunned to encounter the six men still in the living room, and hesitated long enough for all of them to open up at once, making him dance as bullets riddled him from neck to knees.

"Rest in pieces," Killer Combs advised the dead guy, as Hume moved past him down the hallway. He focused on the shared bathroom, the room nearest to him.

He kicked the door in, checked behind the shower curtain, then turned toward the window. Funny that it didn't have a screen to keep the bugs out. Moving closer, Hume peered through the frame and saw the screen in the flower bed below, twisted from being hammered out, dented from someone stepping on it as he cleared the window.

Hume retreated, found the others scanning bedrooms and returning empty-handed. "Spike!" he called. "We lost him."

"What?"

"See for yourself."

O'Connor checked the window and immediately turned the air blue with profanity. When that storm passed, he turned to Hume and asked, "How could we miss him leaving?"

"Don't ask me. I was with you. Sordi and Gounden had the east side covered."

"Shit!"

"What now?" asked Mueller, from the bathroom doorway.

"Now we split," O'Connor answered. "Now I call the man and tell him we screwed up."

"He won't like that," Hume said.

"No shit." O'Connor scowled and hurried past him, out the door.

1

Over the Sierra Nevadas, California

"This is crazy," Jack Grimaldi said. "It's snowing like there's no tomorrow. If I didn't have the instruments—"

Mack Bolan interrupted him. "There won't be a tomorrow for the target, if we wait. The window's small and closing fast."

"What window?" Jack asked. "Can you see anything down there?"

"It doesn't matter. We've been over the terrain."

"From photos, sure. What good is that when you can't see the ground?"

"None at all," said Bolan, "unless you, or one of a half dozen pilots skilled enough to drop me on the spot, is in the cockpit. And you're the best among them."

"Half a dozen?" Jack looked skeptical. "I would've made it three or four."

"Well, there you go then."

"All right, dammit. Flattery will get you anywhere. Almost."

The aircraft was a Cessna 207 Stationair, thirty-two feet long with a thirty-six foot wingspan. Its cruising speed was 136 miles per hour in decent weather, with a maximum range of 795 miles.

Today was far from decent weather, any way you broke it down.

They'd flown out of Modesto City–County Airport, traveling due east. The storm had been barely a whisper in Modesto, but it was kicking ass in the Sierras.

Bolan's chosen landing zone would be bad enough on a clear day, great fangs of granite jutting ten thousand feet or higher, bare and brutal stone on top, flanks covered with majestic pine trees and red fir. A drop directly onto any one of those could easily impale him, or he might get tangled in the rigging of his parachute and hang himself.

In theory, the jump was possible. In practice it was rated very difficult. But in a howling blizzard—for a novice jumper, anyway—it would be tantamount to suicide.

Bolan was not a novice jumper. He had more than his share of combat drops behind him, and had mastered new techniques as they developed, both in uniform and after he'd left military service, following his heart and gut into an endless private war. Today he'd be doing a modified HALO jump, a form of military free fall. The good news: the Cessna's altitude meant there'd be little danger of hypoxia—oxygen starvation—or potentially fatal edema in Bolan's brain or lungs. The bad news: with the blizzard in full cry, he could be whipped around like a mosquito in a blender, lucky if the winds only propelled him miles off course, instead of shredding his ripstop nylon canopy and leaving him to plummet like a stone.

All that to reach the craggy ground below, where the real danger would begin.

"We could go back and get a snowcat," said Grimaldi. "Go in that way. Any small town up here should have one."

Bolan shook his head. "That means an hour's turnaround back to Modesto, grab the four-wheel drive, and what? Pick out the nearest town—"

"I'd land at Groveland," Jack replied. "They've got an airport, they're closer to the mountains—"

"And a snowcat maxes out at fifteen, maybe eighteen miles per hour if the visibility is good enough to risk that. That would mean five hours over mountain roads without the blizzard. The weather we've got now, it could be a day and a half on the road, and I could end up driving over a cliff."

"Still safer than the jump," Grimaldi countered.

"I can handle it. Just get me there."

Frowning, Grimaldi said, "Your wish is my command. Five minutes, give or take."

Bolan got up and started toward the Cessna's starboard double doors, head ducked, crouching in his snow-white insulated jumpsuit. He secured his helmet, ski mask and goggles, and double-checked the main chute on his back and the emergency chute on his chest. He was laden with combat gear to keep himself alive once he was on the ground.

Assuming he reached the ground.

One of the side doors opened easily, caught in a rush of frigid air. The other required more of an effort, the wind pressing it closed, but Bolan got it done.

Outside and down below was a world of swirling white.

Bolan watched and waited for the signal from Grimaldi in the cockpit, answered with a thumbs-up, and leaped into the storm.

The Cessna's slipstream carried Bolan backward, his arms and legs splayed in the proper position for exit from an aircraft, then the plane was gone and gale force winds attacked him like a sentient enemy. His goggles frosted over almost instantly, which wasn't terribly important at the moment, when he couldn't see six feet in front of him regardless, but he'd have to deal with that soon.

The insulated jumpsuit kept him relatively warm, but it wasn't airtight, and the shrieking wind found ways inside: around the collar, through the eyeholes of his mask, around the open ends of Bolan's gloves. The freezing air burned initially, then numbed whatever flesh it found, threatening frostbite.

From thirteen thousand feet, Bolan had about two minutes until he'd hit the ground below. Ninety seconds before he reached four thousand feet and had to deploy his main chute. If dropped any lower without pulling the ripcord, the reserve chute would deploy automatically in time to save his life.

In theory.

At the moment, though, Bolan was spinning like a dreidel in a cyclone, blinded by the snow and frost on his goggles, hoping he could catch a glimpse of the altimeter attached to his left glove. Without it, he'd have to rely on counting seconds in his head. A miscalculation, and he'd be handing his life over to the emergency chute's activation device, hoping it would prevent him from plummeting to certain death in the Sierras.

Bolan brought his right hand to his face with difficulty, scraping at the ice that blurred his goggles. For a second they were clear enough for him to raise his other hand and glance at the altimeter. Eleven thousand feet, which meant he had to count another seventy seconds before deploying his parachute.

And what would happen after that was anybody's guess.

If he didn't survive this jump, it could mean a massacre. A dozen lives, and maybe two or three times more, depended on him without those people knowing it. If he arrived in time, unbroken, and could circumvent the coming siege...

A burst of wind spun Bolan counterclockwise, flipped him over on his back, then righted him again so he was facing the jagged peaks below. He kept counting through the worst of it and reached his silent deadline. Breathing through clenched teeth behind his mask, Bolan reached up to grasp the ripcord's stainless steel D ring.

Instantly, he felt the shock of chute deployment, amplified tenfold by winds that snatched the ripstop canopy, inflated it, then fought to drag their new toy off across the raging sky. Bolan fought back, clutching the lines, knowing his strength was no match for the forces stacked against him.

When the snow cleared for a heartbeat, whipped away as if a giant's hand had yanked a curtain back, Bolan saw frosted granite looming to his left and treetops rising up to skewer him. He'd missed a mountain peak by pure dumb luck and now he had split seconds to correct his course before a lofty pine tree speared him like a chunk of raw meat in a shish kebab.

He hauled hard on his right-hand line, rewarded with a change in course that might be helpful, if it wasn't canceled out by the swirling wind. Bolan was going to hit tree limbs, come what may, but there was still a chance he could escape a crippling impact if his luck held.

As if ordained, the wind changed, whiting out the world below, and he was blind again.

Stout, snow-laden branches started whipping Bolan's legs as he dropped through them. Seconds later, just as he had drawn his knees up to his chest and crossed his arms to protect his face, his parachute snagged something overhead and brought him to a jerking, armpit-chafing halt.

It didn't take a PhD in forestry to realize that he was hung up in a tree.

Craning his neck, he couldn't see the chute above him, only the steering and suspension lines above the slider, disappearing into snow swirl ten or twelve feet overhead. Below him, ditto: whipping snow concealed the distance to the ground.

He assessed his options. Hanging around for any length of time could test the ripstop nylon to its limits. If it had been weakened by a tear, Bolan's weight—or any movements that he made while dangling there—could make things worse and send him plummeting to earth. Conversely, if he couldn't free himself, he would eventually freeze here. Escaping from the parachute itself was not a problem. Each of his harness's shoulder straps was fitted with a quick-release clip for the canopy, while other clips at the chest and groin would free him from the harness altogether. That was easy, but he couldn't rush it; his first false move could finish him. Out here, in this weather, even a fairly short drop could be fatal if he broke his legs and became stranded in the storm.

Bolan remained immobile for a long minute, staring down between his dangling legs until an eddy in the storm gave him a fleeting glimpse of stone and snow-covered ground some ninety feet beneath his boots. A drop from that height would almost surely break his legs and crack his pelvis, maybe drive his shattered femurs up into his body cavity to spear his internal organs. The snow and any fallen pine needles below would cushion him a bit, but likely not enough to avoid crippling injury.

And in this storm, no help within a hundred miles or more, that was a death sentence.

So plummeting was off the table. He would have to climb down—slowly, cautiously—through branches wet and slick with snow and ice, fighting tremors from the cold and the onset of hypothermia.

Bolan considered dropping bits and pieces of his gear—the Steyr AUG assault rifle, at eight pounds loaded; his Beretta 93R, nearly three pounds; his field pack with survival gear, spare magazines and such, tipping the scale at thirty pounds—but balked at that. He didn't plan on losing anything he'd carried with him when he left the Cessna, and whatever Bolan dropped into the storm from where he hung was very likely to be lost.

So he began his treacherous descent, shedding the canopy but not his harness, reaching for the thickest branch that he could see or feel, and hoping it wasn't rotten to the core. When both gloved hands had found their grip, Bolan relaxed his arms enough from the chin-up position for his boots to dangle lower, searching for another branch that would support his weight. When they found purchase, he tested his foothold by slow degrees until he trusted it to hold his weight.

Which wasn't quite the same as holding *him*.

When he released his grip above, the game would change. The gusting wind could knock him from his icy perch, or he could slip. It took the concentration and the balance of a tightrope walker for him to remain upright once both hands left the upper branch, his muscles straining as he slowly sank into a crouch.

Seven or eight feet covered, another eighty-three or so remaining. Bolan knew that as he neared the forest floor, the great tree's branches would become both sparser and fatter, each more difficult to clasp with snow-slick gloves, making a drop more likely. Wind-whipped, cold and tiring, he resumed his painstaking and perilous descent.

2

Washington, D.C., One Day Earlier

Mack Bolan walked among the tourists and joggers at the National Mall, but he hadn't come to see the sights. Somewhere amid the shrines to embattled democracy, among the ambling visitors, another man was watching for him or en route to keep their scheduled rendezvous, a man who might send Bolan to his death.

The risk of meeting here was minimal, by Bolan's normal standard. No one in D.C. knew his face, except the man he'd come to see. Some might recall his name, but if they heard it spoken, it would likely jar a fading memory of his reported death. *Oh,* that *guy,* they'd say. *I heard something about him once. He's long gone.*

And they'd be correct, in part. Mack Bolan had been buried in a ceremony thronged by paparazzi, laid to rest forever with his famous face and fingerprints. The tall man strolling down the southern side of the Reflecting Pool toward the Korean War Veterans Memorial was someone else entirely. But he waged the same long war.

Approaching the memorial, Bolan spotted Hal Brognola, director of the ultrasecret, antiterrorist Sensitive Operations Group standing beneath the steel soldiers.

"I've got something up your alley," Brognola said.

"I got that much on the phone," Bolan replied. "Care to share the details?"

"Did you hear about a shooting in New Mexico two days ago? Las Cruces?"

Bolan frowned in thought. "It doesn't ring a bell."

"Three U.S. marshals KIA," Brognola explained. "It played on CNN for half a day or so."

"Missed it," Bolan replied.

"They were on WITSEC duty, covering a witness set to testify in New York City, day after tomorrow."

"That's a rarity," Bolan said. "Not the coverage, the shooting."

"Right. The service has a pretty solid track record. But things went wrong this time."

"And the witness?"

"Gone."

"Taken?"

"The marshals and the FBI say no. There's evidence—don't ask me what—that he bailed out before the shooters went in gunning for him. DOJ's convinced he's in the wind."

"A dumb move," Bolan said. "Except it saved his life."

"Short term," Brognola said. "Smart money says the shooters will be after him, trying to take him out before the marshals reel him in. Both sides are gambling big time on a win."

"They have to find him first," Bolan observed.

"As it turns out, that's not the problem."

"Oh?"

"We've zeroed in on his location."

"Is it definite?"

"Good as," Brognola said.

"So pick him up."

"Not so easy," Brognola said. "You'll love this part. He's in a monastery."

Bolan cut a glance toward the big Fed but said nothing.

Brognola forged ahead. "You know the rules surrounding sanctuary?"

"It's political," Bolan said.

"Not in this case. Think medieval, as in pilgrims fleeing persecution."

"So, religious."

"Bingo."

"I'm no lawyer, but I've never heard of a statute in the States that recognizes any church's right to harbor fugitives."

"Because there isn't one. We have a free press, though, and when you think about the Bureau's history with sieges, going back to Ruby Ridge and Waco, down to Cliven Bundy in Nevada…well, let's say nobody wants a repetition in the spotlight."

"That's a problem," Bolan granted.

"Plus, if *we* know where he is, the hunters know. They're well-financed and well-connected, through their sponsors."

"Let me guess. The folks your witness planned to put away."

"The very same."

"Can't say I like his odds."

"He needs a hand, no question. I was thinking, maybe yours."

"You think the monks will pass him off to me?"

"They're brothers, technically. And no. You'd have to go in uninvited. Try to make them see the light."

"Because that's so much better than a siege."

"I hope so, anyway."

Bolan stopped short and faced Brognola. "Rewind. I need to hear it from the top."

Brognola launched into how it all began. The missing witness was a CPA, one Arthur Watson, thirty-one and never married, formerly employed by a low-profile megabank, U.S. Global Finance. Bolan had not heard of them before and said so.

"That's no accident," Hal told him. "The outfit is privately owned by some billionaire types—three Americans, one Saudi and a Russian autocrat. There are no other shareholders, so you won't find them on the New York Stock Exchange, NASDAQ or any of the rest. They specialize in large commercial deals worldwide, taking in money from depositors and then recycling it as low-interest loans."

"In other words, a money laundry," Bolan said.

"Big time. Justice has tracked connections to Colombian and Mexican cartels, the Russian mob, the Yakuza, a couple dozen shady government officials from the Balkans and on across the Middle East to Africa. And that's without our homegrown filthy rich—owners of two casino chains, some Wall Street sharks, plus a fellow in Atlanta who just beat a human trafficking indictment when the prosecution's witnesses went belly-up."

"The DOJ knows this, but can't put anything together?"

"Couldn't," Brognola corrected him, "until this Arthur Watson suffered an attack of conscience after five years of cooking their books. From what I hear, he never managed to explain the change of heart. Just tumbled out of bed one morning and decided he should do something about it. He approached the IRS in Philadelphia, where he was living at the time. They handed him to Justice. Watson spilled his guts, and two weeks back we got a sealed indictment on the top three officers at U.S. Global. Sheldon Page, the president, was on vacation in the south of France, and the FBI held off on busting the other two, CEO Cornell Dubois and CFO Reginald Manson, until Page got back Monday night."

"Arrests like that, I would've thought they'd make the news."

"Me, too. But U.S. Global has a ton of influential friends, as you may well imagine. Some of them are in the House and Senate, always grateful for those PAC donations at election time. A federal judge in New York City put a gag order on the proceedings until trial convenes—or was supposed to—day after tomorrow."

"And they've lost the witness."

"Lost and found," Brognola said. "He's with the Brothers of Saint Faustus at their monastery up in the Sierras."

"California."

"More precisely, Mariposa County. The brothers call their hangout Holy Trinity."

"And Justice found him how?"

"He's got a brother at the monastery," Hal replied. "By which I mean blood brother *and* a full-fledged member of the order. Brother Andrew Watson, who is also Arthur's only living kin."

"Well, if you found him—"

"Others can," Brognola said, nodding. "No doubt about it. We don't know any of the hunters, but there's no way they're not on his trail by now."

"Has anyone communicated with the monastery?" Bolan asked.

"Oh, sure. The honcho there—Brother Jerome, he's called the abbot primate—took some calls and tried to plead the Fifth at first, then finally admitted that our guy has joined them as a postulant."

"Which is…?"

"The lowest rung on the monk ladder," Brognola said. "Informal training, getting used to how things work behind the walls, without a uniform or any formal vows. Apprenticeship, you might say, going on for weeks or months, depending on the candidate. If he sticks with it and the monks agree, he graduates to novice and receives his habit, taking on full duties. Make it through a year of that, then he's a junior for the next three years, and finally a brother, if they vote to keep him on."

"It doesn't sound like Watson has four years and change to spare."

"He may not have four days," Brognola said. "For all we know, the shooters from Las Cruces or another crew are moving in right now. The only thing to slow them down would be the weather."

"Weather?"

"Right. Did I mention they've got a blizzard moving in? Supposed to be the worst since 1890-something, in the mountains anyway."

"So the witness has a price tag on his head—"

"Six figures, I was told."

"—the monks won't give him up, the shooters likely have his twenty, and a giant storm is moving in to seal the whole place off like Christmas in the Arctic."

"That's it in a nutshell."

"It sounds impossible," said Bolan.

"Well, I wouldn't say—"

"When do I leave?"

THE NEXT FLIGHT OUT of Ronald Reagan Washington National Airport took off two hours later, bound for Sacramento, California. Bolan caught a break when Brognola informed him Jack Grimaldi was in San Francisco, on some kind of surveillance gig for Stony Man. The pilot volunteered before Bolan could hint around the job's details, although the blizzard gave him pause.

"No sweat," he'd said after a moment. "If they've still got air, we're airborne."

Grimaldi would meet him when the flight landed in Sacramento, with a plane ready to go. He'd drop Bolan into the High Sierras, as close as he could get him to Holy Trinity, weather permitting, then he'd circle back at a prearranged time to pick up the soldier and, if all went well, Arthur Watson.

While Bolan waited for his flight to board at Reagan National, he popped a USB key Brognola had given him into his laptop. He reviewed the photographs and text describing U.S. Global Finance from its inception in the early nineties to the present day, with current assets estimated in the mid twelve figures. That was property and money on the books; no telling what was tucked away in safe deposit boxes or invested overseas.

Sheldon Page, the president, was fifty-one but could have passed for ten years younger, thanks to money, solid genes and plastic surgery. Before his present gig he'd worked for a major bank as a financial counselor, then jumped ship with his richest clients when U.S. Global started up. He was on first-name terms with several presidents south of the border, though he kept his distance—in the public eye, at least—from the leaders of their top cartels.

The CEO, Cornell Dubois, was forty-eight and twice divorced, a Harvard legacy who'd gone from graduation to the second-largest law firm in Manhattan, keeping big-time clients out of trouble with the IRS, the SEC and anybody else who sniffed around their fortunes. That experience had prepped him for the position he held at U.S. Global's helm, leading a bicoastal life with junkets out of country when the need arose. Fluent in Spanish, French and Russian, he could wheel and deal in something like a hundred countries with the best of them.

Reginald Manson was the chief financial officer and youngest of the three at forty-six, a bachelor who played the field when there was time between his workload and his private passion, which was big-game hunting. Shooters' magazines and websites showed him standing over carcasses—the African "big five" and other species standing on the knife's edge of extinction—with a rifle in his hands and a smug look on his face. Before landing at U.S. Global he had worked for five top banks in various capacities, leaving each post with glowing letters of recommendation.

The fourth man Bolan met in Brognola's files was Brad Kemper, chief of U.S. Global's security division. He was twenty-nine, an Iraqi war vet and short-time LAPD officer, forced to resign after a series of brutality complaints climaxed with a dicey shooting, costing the city seven figures in compensatory damages. From there, he'd jumped to corporate security, working with a private military company that banked a bundle from Afghanistan and was suspected of coordinating drug shipments through Turkey to the West. That may have helped Kemper with his next move, to U.S. Global, where he'd caught the guy who hired him skimming funds—or framed him for it, as the case might be. Whichever, Kemper had replaced the tarnished chief and held his post today.

It would have been Kemper, Bolan thought, who'd fielded hunters to dispose of Arthur Watson. He would not have led the team himself, too risky, but the shooters would be dancing to his tune. If all else failed, Bolan thought Kemper might be worth a closer look, maybe through the crosshairs of a rifle's scope.

Sacramento, California

JACK GRIMALDI WAS waiting in the terminal as promised when Bolan disembarked The pilot looked the same as ever, suntanned, just a trifle cocky in the way of men who've overcome the handicap of gravity and earn their living in the clouds. His grasp was firm as they shook hands. Grimaldi got right to business.

"I bagged a Cessna 207." he told Bolan. "Not one of the old ones, but a fairly new production model."

"Fairly new?"

"Early two thousands," Grimaldi replied. "No worries about getting where we need to go."

"Except the storm," Bolan said.

"Well, there's that. We won't know whether the National Weather Service is overstating it or not until we're in the middle of it."

"Great."

"We'll play it by ear, right?" Grimaldi suggested. "I don't wanna die any more than you do. If you can't drop in safely, we'll try something else."

Except Bolan knew there would be nothing else. He'd either jump into the storm for Arthur Watson, or he'd have to sit it out. Ground travel through the High Sierras would be deadly slow, if it was even possible. He was already starting out behind the field, no way of knowing where the hunters were, what kind of heat they had, or how they would approach their prey.

Bolan had searched Holy Trinity on the internet while he was passing over Kansas. The place looked ancient, like a fortress from a movie about medieval times, when knighthood was in flower and encroaching armies laid siege to a rival's keep for weeks or months on end.

Neither Bolan nor the hunters had that kind of time, of course. The shooters would be aware that their mark could change his mind again and get permission for the FBI to land at Holy Trinity, extract him and return him to New York to testify. In that case, there would be no payday, and the failed hunters might find their own heads on the chopping block.

The flight from Sacramento to Modesto was a short hop, sixty-odd miles, under thirty minutes at the Cessna's cruising speed. They landed and refueled with ample daylight left to make the drop, Bolan trusting Grimaldi to have checked his parachute first-hand. Bolan strapped it on when they were airborne, heading east toward a wall of gray and white that was the blizzard blanketing the Golden State's main mountain range.

And all that he could do was tough it out from there, bearing in mind the cost of failure if he turned back or was otherwise prevented from completing his assignment. Arthur Watson was the target, but it didn't take a West Point graduate to figure out that U.S. Global's mercs would leave no witnesses alive. From what Bolan had read online, there were about three dozen full-fledged monks at Holy Trinity, plus a handful of postulants, juniors and novices. Call it forty-plus to be on the safe side, and write them all off if the mercs got inside with no one to stop them.

What could one man do?

That was the question Mack Bolan had fielded from day one of his private war against the Mafia, through combat on a global scale against the predators who menaced civilized society. His answer, then and now, remained unchanged.

One man could do his best. If he was trained, experienced and willing, that could make the difference between a massacre of innocents and a defeat for evil. Permanent elimination of the threat was never part of the equation. Every battle was a thing unto itself. The enemies you killed today would be replaced tomorrow.

But one man could make his mark, all right. In blood.

3

Sierra Nevadas, California

Descending from the ancient pine tree was a slow and awkward process. Bolan relied mostly on touch, as swirling snow and frosted goggles prevented him from seeing more than a few feet in any direction. Swiping the goggles clear meant letting go of a branch, a dicey proposition, but he risked it periodically to keep himself from being completely blinded.

Another problem: Bolan's high-topped jump boots were designed to save his ankles from a break or sprain on landing, and for marching the necessary distance to his goal, but their lug soles quickly caked with frozen snow, putting him at even more risk for a fatal slip.

He felt exposed up in the tree, knowing that anyone who'd seen him drop could wait below for an easy shot and pick him off, no problem. On the upside, Bolan thought he was at least a mile from Holy Trinity. That meant a grueling hike through knee-deep snow, but it also limited the possibility of encountering an enemy.

If there were shooters in the neighborhood, they would be headed for the monastery, bent on finishing their work and getting out again before the storm trapped them there. Meeting a hostile party here and now would be a fluke, defying logic and the odds, though it was not out of the question.

As for the High Sierras' natural predators, they would be deep in hibernation or long departed for warmer elevations by now, or at the very least huddled in shelter from the storm. The checklist wasn't long to start with—mountain lions, bears, coyotes, rattlesnakes. If he met killers here, they'd be the worst that nature had to offer: human beings.

And the Executioner was used to those.

A heavy-laden branch snapped under Bolan's feet. One second he was balanced, pausing to wipe his goggles, and then his perch dropped out from under him, its *crack* sounding as loud as rifle fire.

Sixty feet of empty air yawned underneath him, broken only by the branches that would bruise and break him as he fell. Bolan had one hand on a limb, and he felt his fingers slipping through the slush. His free hand found another one in time, but only just, and dangling there in space, his shoulder sockets burning, Bolan knew he was in trouble.

He would have to find another branch to stand on, then use as his next handhold, which meant moving closer to the pine's trunk, and inching to his left or right until he found another limb to take his weight.

A bare inch at a time, he worked his way toward the trunk. It was too stout for him to wrap his arms around, but with one hand on the branch overhead and the other hugging the tree, Bolan was hopeful he could extend a leg to the left or right and find another perch before he lost his grip and fell. The pine's bark, normally as rough as ancient alligator hide, was glazed with ice that made it slicker than a polished fireman's pole.

It took the better part of ten minutes to pull it off, each minute giving an advantage to his enemies if they were closing in on Holy Trinity. Even if they weren't— say that the storm had overtaken them in the foothills somewhere and prevented them from getting to the monastery—time still mattered. Bolan had to find the place, wangle a way inside, find Arthur Watson and convince him that he had to finish up the job he'd signed on for.

All that, and then get Watson out alive through snow that might be chest-deep by then, with no flat, open ground to let Grimaldi land, if he could even fly in the blizzard. Did Watson have cold weather gear? The monks, presumably, would stay inside when weather canceled gardening or other chores, huddling by their simple fires or meditating in their Spartan living quarters. Bolan would carry Watson out swaddled in homespun blankets if he had to, but he didn't like the odds of surviving that scenario.

Bolan's foot found the branch he had been searching for and he shifted his weight forward, still bracing against the trunk. When he was certain the limb would hold him, he swung his other leg onto it, leaning into the tree for stability. He rested briefly, and when he could feel his arms and hands again, resumed his grueling descent toward whatever awaited him below.

THE SNOWCAT WAS A Thiokol 601 Trackmaster, designed originally for the U.S. military and adapted over time for various civilian tasks. It was bright orange—or had been, before snow and ice had crusted over it—and reminded Spike O'Connor of a school bus jacked up to accommodate tank treads. The heater worked all right; in fact, he felt a little sweaty, packed in with eleven other guys. The heavy-duty windshield wipers were another story, snow-clotted and leaving more behind than they were clearing on each pass. Not that it mattered in the near-whiteout conditions they were facing.

Denikin handled the driving. Who better to navigate a winter wasteland than a Russian who had done part of his Spetsnaz training in Siberia?

O'Connor left him to it. The other members of his team, clad in all-white uniforms, were from Germany, South Africa, Australia, Israel, Italy, England and the USA, but each possessed that look common to men who had been tested in the fire of battle and proved themselves. Their weapons had been chosen for utility and uniformity. O'Connor and the seven others carried Galil MAR assault rifles, the compact models with folding stocks and eight-inch barrels that still provided the parent rifle's full firepower, feeding 5.56 mm NATO ammunition from thirty-five-round magazines at seven hundred rounds per minute in full auto mode. Two men packed Benelli M4 Super 90 shotguns, twelve-gauge semiautomatics with collapsible stocks, loading six rounds in the magazine plus one up the spout. Two others, their snipers, carried Accuracy International Arctic Warfare rifles topped with Schmidt & Bender 3-12x50 PM II P telescopic sights. They fed

7.62 mm NATO ammunition from ten-round detachable box magazines, but O'Connor's marksmen rarely needed second shots to do their job.

As far as handguns went, he'd left it up to each individual, half of them choosing Glocks, most of the rest drawing various SIG Sauer models. The lone exception was their German, Kurt Mueller, who carried a Walther P1 identical in its appearance to the old P38 his forebears might have carried into battle during World War II. Nostalgia, maybe, or brand loyalty to the Fatherland.

O'Connor was frustrated by the snowcat. They were grinding along at ten miles per hour at best through the drifts and high winds, but at least they were still on course, their vehicle's GPS device providing turn-by-turn navigation to Denikin. There were no cliffs in the immediate vicinity, and even if the Trackmaster veered off the narrow, snowed-in road a bit, its treads would bring them back in line. O'Connor's major worry now was fallen trees, which could prevent the snowcat from proceeding and leave them on foot, with five miles left to go.

If that happened, so be it. They had a job to do and had been paid half in advance. The snafu in New Mexico had been a setback, but O'Connor wasn't dwelling on it. If they failed this time, however, then they might as well die trying. Their employers were like elephants, forgetting nothing, and they didn't know the meaning of forgiveness.

This was do or die at thirty-five below and dropping, arm's length visibility and winds that forced a strong man to hunch over.

This time we get it right, O'Connor told himself, or we're not going home.

WHEN BOLAN'S BOOTS met solid ground he stopped and leaned back against the pine tree's massive trunk to get his bearings and catch his breath. The air he inhaled through his woven mask was frigid, making his throat burn, while the hairs inside his covered nostrils had a crisp and brittle feel. His arms and legs were strained from the descent, but there was no time to relax, no place to sit or lie down in the snow, which was more than knee deep and was accumulating rapidly.

He had to push on. Forty-odd lives depended on his perseverance, along with the indictment of three parasites who had grown bloated on the blood of innocents.

Before proceeding, Bolan shed his parachute harness, took a lightweight parka from his field pack and slipped into it, then removed a GPS device from one of his jumpsuit's pockets. Switching it on, he waited for the LED display to orient him in a world of blinding white. The screen told him he was 1.5 miles south-southwest of Holy Trinity.

He spent another moment checking out his hardware: a Steyr AUG assault rifle with white polymer furniture and translucent double-column magazine; a Beretta 93R selective fire machine pistol; six M26 fragmentation grenades; and a Mark I trench knife with a seven-inch blade and a brass knuckle handle. When he'd verified the items were in their proper places, all undamaged, Bolan struck off through the drifts.

Fighting the wind, which was against him, and the snow, which made each step feel as if his feet were mired in tar, he strode toward Holy Trinity. Flakes were settling on his hood and shoulders, clinging to his sleeves and gloves. He'd kept his tinted goggles on, to guard against snow blindness and the biting cold, and he scanned the white landscape incessantly, watching out for movement and for any sign of tracks.

So far he seemed to be alone.

No reason why the hunters should have come this way, of course. In fact, he highly doubted that they would have jumped into the mountains as he had. He figured there had to be a team, as in Las Cruces, when they'd taken the U.S. Marshals down and missed their prize. Multiple jumpers in the storm likely would have been separated, maybe scattered over rugged miles, losing precious time while they regrouped, assuming all of them survived.

So, Bolan calculated, they'd be coming overland. The question was *when*.

He'd scouted the terrain as best he could, with satellite photography Brognola had provided, learning that a single narrow, winding road linked Holy Trinity to the outside world. On clear days, it would take a driver in a 4x4 about three hours to reach the nearest town, Groveland, 3,136 feet above sea level and a population of just over six hundred. A small town, obviously, boasting one main drag and two hotels competing for the tourist trade, no doubt including someplace where determined men with cash in hand could rent or buy adequate transportation to the high country.

Not simple SUVs in this weather. Land transport to Holy Trinity on a day like this meant snowmobiles or something larger that could flatten three-foot drifts and cling to icy pavement without mishap.

Snowmobiles were loud. As for the larger possibilities…

Bolan stopped short, blinking behind his goggles. Ahead of him, partially obscured by blowing powder, a wall stretched as far as he could see from right to left. It was approximately twelve feet high, no razor wire on top, just ice and snow to make it slippery.

Something he'd anticipated.

Dropping his field pack, Bolan opened it and reached inside.

BROTHER THOMAS LOVED the snow. Its chill and silence stilled his memories of the chaotic desert hell where he had served three tours of duty among people who despised him, wished him dead and did their level best to make it so. The hush a deep snow brought to Holy Trinity was music to his ears and to his soul.

In truth, though, Brother Thomas loved all seasons at the monastery. He was pleased—not proud, worst of the deadly sins—to be a member of the small community devoted to communion with the Lord and greater understanding of His plan. The brotherhood demanded nothing of him that involved deciding who should live or die, walk free or be confined pending interrogation by the faceless men who called the shots outside the monastery's walls.

Snow shovel duty was his lot this afternoon, a task that might seem futile with the storm still raging, but it kept him fit and served his brothers as they went about their daily tasks. It was an hour past None—one of the Little Hours, celebrated with psalms at 3:00 p.m.—and Brother Thomas had three paths to clear before Supper at half-past five. Someone else would likely have to do the job all over again before Vespers, the day's last Major Hour, when the monks gathered to celebrate sunset.

As he began to clear a path serving the refectorium—what would have been the mess hall in his bygone military sojourn—Brother Thomas warmed from the exertion. Work was deemed a privilege at Holy Trinity, not something to be borne, but rather celebrated as a service to the brotherhood and to their Lord. It varied with the seasons, gardening from late spring into early fall, woodcutting for the stoves and fireplaces, whatever maintenance the monastery might require year-round. The best part was that none of it involved divesting any other soul of life or liberty.

The path was almost clear when Brother Thomas heard a sharp metallic clinking. It had come from somewhere to his left, in the direction of the monastery's high west wall, and was alarming in its unfamiliarity. He stopped and listened, but the sound was not repeated. Leaning on his shovel, Brother Thomas pondered whether he should put it out of mind or go investigate.

It's likely nothing, he decided. But what if it was something that required repair?

Taking his shovel with him, Brother Thomas moved in the direction of the sound, his boot tracks quickly fading as snow filled them up. His view of the west wall improved as he advanced, but snowy gusts still masked it. Was there something *moving* on the wall, descending toward the garden plot inside?

A trespasser, dressed all in white, his movements deft and spider-like.

Brother Thomas clutched his shovel like a weapon.

As the man in white touched down, boots crunching into snow, Brother Thomas called out, "Who are you?"

INSTEAD OF ANSWERING, Bolan slowly turned, his right hand drifting automatically to the Steyr AUG's smooth pistol grip.

"You need to answer me," the same voice said.

The man who stood before him was approximately Bolan's height, possibly bulkier beneath his thick parka. Below the coat's hem, Bolan saw the dark sweep of a snow-dusted robe over black rubber boots. Gloved hands clutched a broad shovel as if it were an ax. The man's ebony face was grim but handsome.

"Names aren't important," Bolan said.

"Then you won't have a problem sharing yours."

"I've come to help you."

"With your handy Steyr AUG?"

The brother knew his weapons, and he had a military bearing—feet apart, the shovel held up defensively.

"It's for protection," Bolan replied.

"Uh-huh. Against what, the abominable snowman?"

"Trouble's coming."

"Looks to me like it's already here."

"I'm telling you—"

"No weapons on the monastery grounds. You need to give it up."

Bolan considered that, released the Steyr's pistol grip and raised his free right hand. "I'll trade it for a face-to-face," he said. "Take me to see Brother Jerome."

The shovel-bearer frowned. "You know the abbot primate?"

"Haven't had the pleasure yet," Bolan replied. "But I've got news he needs to hear."

It was the monk's turn to consider his options. Finally, he said, "I take the rifle and you walk ahead of me."

It was a gamble, but the other choices ran against the grain. "Okay."

"Unsling it, hold it by the telescopic with your left hand and pass it over to me. Any fancy moves, you get to sample my Paul Bunyan imitation."

"With a shovel?"

"You'd be surprised how sharp it is, from all those years of scraping ice."

"I'll take your word for it." He passed the Steyr over, and the monk received it with respect and confidence. "You know your weapons," Bolan said.

"Used to, but I still recall enough. This way." He gestured with the Steyr's muzzle and Bolan preceded him across the courtyard to a path partially cleared of snow. The monk set down his shovel there, leaving both hands free for the AUG.

Two minutes later, they were standing at a massive, ironbound wooden door. "Go on," the brother said. "It isn't locked."

Bolan opened the door and passed into the lobby of a stone-and-mortar building. The floor under his dripping boots was gray tile. In front of them a broad staircase ascended to the second floor.

"Upstairs," the monk directed. "Then the first door to your right."

Bolan began to climb the stairs. A younger brother met them halfway up and hurried on his way after he saw the gun. When Bolan reached the second floor, he turned right, stopped and waited for the monk's next move.

He knocked, keeping his eyes on Bolan the whole time. A deep voice on the other side said, "Enter!"

"Go ahead," the monk said.

Bolan stepped into an office with a simple desk and wooden chairs, cheap filing cabinets against one wall. The setup seemed out of place beneath a twelve-foot ceiling. Multicolored light came through a stained glass window set in stone behind the desk. Christ in a garden of olive trees. Even without a clear sky behind it, the window was impressive, ancient-looking, wrought with care.

A tall man in a drab brown habit rose from where he had been seated at the desk, examining the new arrivals through a pair of wire-rimmed glasses. "What on earth is this?" he asked the brother holding Bolan's AUG.

"He came over the wall, Father," the monk replied. "With this."

"A firearm."

"Yes, Father."

The abbot turned to Bolan. "Who are you?"

Rather than debate it, Bolan used the name printed on the ID he'd left with Jack Grimaldi. "Matthew Cooper."

"Named for a disciple?"

"Not that I'm aware of."

"Brother Thomas," said the abbot, "I'll relieve you of your burden."

"Father—"

"Please. And wait outside."

It was the monk's turn to obey, passing the Steyr to his boss, shooting a warning glance at Bolan as he left and closed the door.

Brother Jerome studied the rifle for a moment, placed it on his desk and said, "I won't ask why you've come. It's sadly obvious."

"Or maybe not," Bolan replied.

Brother Jerome cocked one gray eyebrow at him, clearly skeptical. "We have a visitor among us, claiming sanctuary. He desires to be a postulant. Intruders from his old life seek to take him from us. You are one of them."

"You're half-right," Bolan granted. "But I'm not the only one who's coming, and I'm on your side."

"We don't need men with guns to help us do the Lord's work, Mr. Cooper."

"There are others coming," Bolan said again. "They've killed already, would've taken your visitor long before he got here if they hadn't missed him. He got away once. Between your setup and the storm, I can't imagine he'll be lucky twice."

"Who do you represent?" Brother Jerome demanded.

"No one who'll acknowledge me," Bolan replied. "We're off the record here."

"I see. Perhaps I should inform you that I've spoken to the FBI, the U.S. Marshals Service, and someone claiming to be a deputy attorney general. I have told them all the same thing. Sanctuary is a sacred principle that I am not prepared to violate."

"That's why I'm here, and not a SWAT team," Bolan said. "Nobody's looking for another Waco, but the men tracking your guest are only paid to do one thing—and I can promise you they don't leave any witnesses."

Brother Jerome stood silent for a moment, fingertips pinning the Steyr to his desktop. Finally, he said, "The choice cannot be mine. Brother Thomas!"

In a second flat, the monk who had delivered Bolan stood beside him. "Father?"

"Please fetch Brother Andrew and the postulant at once. I need to speak with both of them."

4

Modesto, California

The storm chased Jack Grimaldi back to town, whipping his rented Cessna 207 all the way. He landed none the worse for wear and set about refueling before he tied the aircraft down. The blizzard's trailing edge was rattling shrubbery around the airport terminal, but snow was limited to tiny flakes, like dandruff, which vanished on contact with the pavement.

The guy who'd checked Grimaldi's license and his rental paperwork came out to meet him, flicking nervous glances at the clouds. "Did she treat you all right?"

"Sweet as candy," Grimaldi replied."

"Think you'll be going up again?"

Grimaldi deflected with a question of his own. "I've got it through tomorrow, right?"

"Right, right. I only wondered, with the storm and all—"

"I'm waiting on a call," Grimaldi said. "It comes, I go. Till then, she's battened down."

"Yessir. Okay."

The guy veered off and left him, doubtless going to inspect the plane. Grimaldi had already signed off on insurance that would reimburse the owner with a new plane if he wrecked it, whether he survived or not. Still, he understood the natural, paternal feeling the man had for the machine that earned his living for him.

Grimaldi got into his Chevy TrailBlazer, another rental, and left the airport, heading north with his stomach growling. It might have struck some people as bizarre, going to eat while his friend was facing God knew what in the Sierras, but his body needed fuel to function properly for his next flight. And for all Grimaldi knew, Bolan would need more than just a ride when he arrived at their rendezvous.

Grimaldi found a mom-and-pop Mexican restaurant, went in and ordered up their biggest combination platter, one of damn near every item on the menu. He washed it down with coffee, black, and kept it coming throughout the meal. When he was done, he tipped well, not concerned about the young waitress remembering his face.

No one was likely to come asking questions later, sniffing down his trail. If Bolan was successful, they'd be covered seven ways from Sunday. If he failed, well, chances were they'd both be dead.

Returning to the airport, Grimaldi listened to the weather report on the radio. No letup in the blizzard was expected for the next eighteen to twenty-four hours, at least. High winds, unseasonable snowfall, yada-yada. There was nothing new, so he gave up and switched it off.

Grimaldi thought of calling Stony Man, asking if anyone had traced the hunting party they assumed was headed for the monastery, but he scrubbed that thought. Unless the farm located them precisely, there was nothing more to learn. And if that happened, *they'd* be calling *him* to share the news.

He parked the TrailBlazer beside the rental company's hangar and walked back to the terminal, wind plucking at his jeans and jacket as he crossed the tarmac.

The sat-phone in his jacket pocket was a cold dead weight. It was too soon for a call, of course, and unless he heard otherwise, the plan was to return to the monastery at dusk. Grimaldi still had hours before he had to go up again. If Bolan had survived the jump and landed more or less on target, without mishaps on the ground, he should be close to Holy Trinity by now, maybe inside.

Grimaldi didn't envy Bolan the task ahead of him.

Holy Trinity Monastery

BOLAN STOOD UP when Brother Thomas entered again, ushering two more men into the abbot primate's office. One of them was Arthur Watson, little changed from the mug shot Brognola had provided, except for added worry lines around his mouth and eyes. The other man, dressed identically to Brother Thomas in a plain brown habit, had to be the older sibling, Brother Andrew.

Brother Jerome addressed the new arrivals without rising. "This uninvited visitor," he said, nodding at Bolan, is Matthew Cooper, or purports to be. He comes in peace, supposedly, to speak for others he cannot identify, but brings a weapon to our doorstep."

Weapons, Bolan silently corrected, glad that the parka hid his sidearm, frag grenades and knife. The Watson brothers stared at Bolan, at his rifle, then back at him again. Their faces reflected equal measures of concern, though Arthur's eyes held fear, as well.

"I'm here to help you," Bolan told the fugitive from WITSEC. "Men are coming for you. If I found you, they can, too."

Arthur glanced at Brother Jerome. "Father?"

"Speak freely here," the abbot primate said.

Frowning, Arthur turned back to Bolan. "Who sent you here?"

"Call it a government agency and let it go at that."

"I've told Father Jerome that I won't testify. He's passed that on repeatedly. You can't arrest me here."

"I can't but someone else could. There's no law in the States that recognizes sanctuary in a church."

"All right, you're not here to arrest me. Then what *are* you here for?"

"Call me an expediter. I can get you out of here, with any luck, before the U.S. Global team shows up and blows the house down."

Watson shook his head emphatically. "I don't believe they'd try that. There would be too much exposure."

"They've already tried it," Bolan said. "You know about Las Cruces, right?"

Confusion creased the runner's face. "Las Cruces? What about it?"

"So, you haven't heard?"

"Heard *what?*"

"They took out your security detail. Three marshals dead. Looks like you missed them by an eyelash there."

"My God!" The postulant collapsed into a straight-backed wooden chair. "Forgive me, Father."

But Brother Jerome was focusing on Bolan now. "These murderers you say are coming," he began. "Why don't police simply arrest them for the crimes they've already committed?"

"Easily said," Bolan replied. "So far, no one knows who or where they are, how many are involved or how they're traveling. If they're already in the mountains, which I'm betting that they are, the law can't reach them through the storm. But they can still reach you."

"And what, pray tell, do you suggest?"

The Sierra Nevadas

"WE SHOULD BE THERE within the hour," Denikin announced, fighting the snowcat's wheel as the machine dipped to the right.

About damn time, thought Tyrone Jackson, but he kept his face deadpan. He felt a little claustrophobic in the crowded snowcat, but he wouldn't let it show.

He had a reputation to protect, though granted, it was not a good one. He'd been pressured to resign from the LAPD and its SWAT team, where the brass claimed he'd racked up a record number of complaints about excessive force. The last straw was a "questionable" shooting, and Jackson had been blackballed from his chosen field of law enforcement at the age of twenty-five. He'd worked security for eighteen months, but couldn't stand the comedown to a lousy rent-a-cop, and had decked his supervisor one night when the little weasel used a slur against him after Jackson had shown up late to work. The company considered pressing charges, but they gave that up when Jackson threatened legal action for discrimination, and he got a two-month severance deal instead.

From there, he'd joined a private military company, despite the fact that he had never served in any uniform except blue serge. His record as a SWAT team sniper, even with its blemishes, had helped him land the gig, but another "incident" got him canned, this time without the racial slurs or any silver parachute.

His luck had turned when U.S. Global sent a guy around, a few days after he was fired, to make Jackson an offer. As he'd quickly learned, they weren't exactly kosher when it came to the law, and that was fine with him. This was his third mission with the company, the first time he'd committed first degree murder on U.S. soil, and Jackson found it didn't bother him.

Not one damn bit.

But he was getting sick and tired of snow.

The team was fine, as far as that went. O'Connor was the honcho, and they'd worked together pretty well so far, unless you counted letting Arthur Freakin' Watson get away in New Mexico.

As far as Jackson was concerned, he could look up "shitstorm" in the dictionary and find a snapshot of the meeting where they got their asses reamed for that snafu. Three U.S. marshals smoked, the DOJ blowing a gasket over it, and Watson in the wind. It made the L.A. inquisition after Jackson shot a hostage in a standoff situation look like *Happy Days*.

But what the hell, he'd nailed the hostage-taker at the same time, hadn't he?

Now here he was, packed like a sweaty sardine in the snowcat with eleven other guys, all strapped in and ready for a shot at self-redemption, while they rumbled through a blizzard at a snail's pace, headed for another massacre. This one, he knew, was going to be worse than Las Cruces, but at least he didn't have to sweat their targets shooting back.

He had his sniper's rifle in a padded case, to keep the Schmidt & Bender scope from being jostled after it was zeroed in. Same thing with former Special Forces marksman Deadeye Blake's gun. The others wore their MARs and shotguns across their shoulders or in their laps, ready to rock and roll.

Snipers couldn't be too careful with their tools.

The thought made Jackson smirk, and Blake leaned across the narrow aisle and asked him, "What's so funny?"

"My ass. It's getting numb."

"We're almost there," Blake said.

And then the snowcat shuddered to a stop. Up front, the Russian said, "We have problem."

Holy Trinity Monastery

"IDEALLY, I'D TAKE Mr. Watson out of here and leave the rest of you in peace," Bolan said in answer to the abbot primate's question about his plans.

Brother Jerome replied, "But if these others are already on the way—"

"They won't accept your word that he's moved on," Bolan said, finishing his thought. "And once you've seen them, you're a liability."

Some of the ruddy color faded from the abbot's face. "I can't believe—"

"Believe it," Bolan interrupted him. "How often do you go down for supplies?"

The sudden change of topics appeared to confuse Brother Jerome. "Approximately once a month. Less often in the winter, when the roads close and we stock up in advance. How is that relevant?"

"It gives the shooters lead time," Bolan said. "They can be in and out, long gone and scattered to the wind, before somebody in the real world wonders why they haven't heard from you, and comes around to check."

"This *is* the real world, Mr. Cooper. Prayer and meditation—"

"No offense intended," Bolan said. "My point is that it won't do any good for me to take Watson and go. You're still in danger, either way."

"Excuse me." Arthur Watson spoke up. "You're talking like I've already agreed to go somewhere with you. I haven't. You're a stranger out of nowhere, telling stories. You could be from U.S. Global and the rest of it could all be lies."

"Fair enough." Bolan turned to the abbot primate. "Call the nearest TV station's news desk. Ask about the marshals in Las Cruces. They can brief you on—"

"We do not have a telephone," Brother Jerome informed him. "Separation from the world outside is central to our doctrine. We have a shortwave radio for emergencies, but it's not functioning. The storm."

"Terrific," Bolan said. "How are you set for self-defense?"

O'CONNOR SQUINTED INTO driving snow and saw the problem right away. A tree—no, two trees, both fairly massive—had fallen up ahead, their huge trunks blocking the narrow access road.

What were the odds of two trees dropping just that way, precisely in the snowcat's path? O'Connor didn't have the first clue, but he didn't like it.

"Lock and load," he ordered. "Everybody out, and keep your eyes peeled. This could be a setup."

He was first out of the vehicle, the others close behind him, forming a defensive circle in the cold white wilderness. O'Connor, Denikin and Combs moved forward to inspect the trees, checking them for any evidence that they had been hacked down by human hands to form a roadblock.

"This one came out of the ground," Blake said, jabbing the muzzle of his MAR toward twisted roots clotted with frozen dirt, resembling the fat arms of a giant squid.

"And this one snapped," Denikin said. "A ragged break. No saw."

"All right." O'Connor guessed each tree weighed tons on its own, with further tons of snow making them top-heavy. It wasn't unusual for trees like this to topple in these conditions. These likely weren't the first, and wouldn't be the last.

"Think we can move 'em?" Blake asked. "Maybe with the snowcat?"

"Is possible," said Denikin. "In theory. We have a winch and chains, but each of these weighs more than our machine. We run a risk of damage to the motor, the transmission, who can say?"

O'Connor didn't like the sound of that. It would mean hiking to the monastery, then one hell of a long walk down to the lowlands through the worst snowstorm he'd

ever seen. It could take days, and they had no food or
camping gear.

"Didn't you ever haul trees in Siberia, someplace
like that?" Blake asked Denikin.

"I am not a lumberjack," the Russian answered.
"*They* use cranes and special trucks to move trees this
size."

"But still—"

O'Connor cut Blake off. "We only need to clear the
road and let the cat squeeze through. Think we could
muscle it?"

Denikin shook his head. "A hundred men, maybe,
could move one. Maybe not."

"So what now, Chief?" Blake asked.

Ignoring him, O'Connor asked the Russian, "How
much farther to the monastery?"

"GPS says one-point-seven miles. Not so far to drive,
but—"

"Since we've got no choice, we're walking," O'Connor
said.

"Shit," Blake said. "I was afraid of that."

"A little hike," O'Connor told him. "Thing you ought
to be afraid of is what happens if we screw this up a
second time. When Global fires you—"

"We stay fired," Blake said. "I know."

O'Connor waddled back through thigh-deep snow
to reach the others. "Listen up!" he said. "The snowcat can't get past this barricade. We leave it here and
hike the last bit, less than two miles left to go. We do
our business, walk back here, then take the cat down to
Groveland and clear out. Two minutes to collect whatever gear you left on board before we lock it up."

There was some grumbling, but no one argued with

him. They all knew the penalty for failure, and none of them had a better plan on tap. They cleared the cat of field packs and were ready to go in well under two minutes.

"Right, then," said O'Connor. "Move it out."

"The Lord is our defender," Brother Jerome said. "We are not combatants here."

"And if you had to be?" Bolan pressed.

"It is irrelevant. We have no weapons."

"Everyone has weapons, even if they have to improvise. You'll find them in the kitchen, maybe in a toolshed."

"You portray these evil-doers as professional assassins. I assume you're speaking from experience?"

Bolan let that one pass. "They may pretend to be negotiating at first, before they drop the hammer, but I guarantee they won't leave anyone behind to talk about them when they're gone."

"They'll be well trained, experienced," the abbot primate said.

"No doubt," Bolan agreed.

"In which case, we have no defense against them other than our faith."

"How does that normally work out for martyrs?" Bolan asked.

"Our Savior Jesus Christ commands us to love our enemies and pray for those who persecute us."

"Isn't suicide a mortal sin?" Bolan inquired.

"Submission to the will of God is not equivalent to suicide," Brother Jerome replied.

"So you'll just stand and take it, all of you?"

"If I can speak to them, persuade them of their sin—"

Bolan had heard enough. "Will you at least put Watson someplace where he'll be hard to find?"

"I'm standing right here," the WITSEC runaway insisted. "With all respect, Father, I should have some say as to what becomes of me."

Bolan cut in. "You brought this trouble with you when you came here. Now, instead of one neck on the line, there's what? Thirty? Forty?"

"Thirty-seven," said the abbot primate. "Yourself excluded."

Bolan had no idea how many guns were on the way. If the odds worked out to about three to one, the monks armed with kitchen knives and shovels, they might stand a chance against a force of eleven or twelve. But even a handful of automatic weapons would put their enemies at an extreme advantage. Bolan would have to do his best to take them out with what firepower he had.

"All right," he said at last. "I'll handle it myself."

Brother Jerome, while roughly Bolan's height, still had a knack for looking down his nose. "I can't allow that," he decreed. "This is the house of God, on hallowed ground. I won't permit it to become a battlefield."

"You say that like you've got a choice," Bolan replied.

"I am the abbot primate!"

"Titles. You won't defend yourself, but now you dictate what you won't allow? How's that work?"

Putting on a frown, Brother Jerome leaned forward, planting both hands on the Steyr AUG. "If necessary, I will order you restrained, as peaceably as may be possible."

Bolan stepped closer to the desk, holding the abbot primate's level gaze. "Good luck with that," he said.

The staring contest lasted half a minute, maybe less. Brother Jerome blinked first and moved back, standing with his gaze downcast as Bolan claimed his weapon from the desktop.

"If you won't help me," Bolan said, "stay out of my way."

5

Bolan tried his sat phone from the monastery's lobby and got nothing but a burst of static for his trouble. Curious to find out if the tons of stone around him were blocking his signal, he opened the huge front door, stepped far enough outside to try it from the snow-blown porch, and got the same result. Cut off from any contact with the outside world for now, he pocketed the phone, pulled on his insulated mask and gloves, and started his recon of Holy Trinity's grounds.

He'd seen the place from above, in satellite photos, and Brognola's dossier had included some schematic drawings from the architect who'd planned the sprawling structure back in 1948. Bolan assumed the major chambers indicated there—the nave and transepts, the refectory, the kitchen and the mess hall, the infirmary and two chapels—would still be serving their initial purposes. There were many smaller rooms in the plans that Bolan assumed were used for storage, prayer and sleep, but that would matter only if his enemies broke through and he had to defend the monastery from the inside, room to room.

He hoped it wouldn't come to that, but he was on his own, policing thirty-odd acres and a three-story building in near-zero visibility. The first thing Bolan did was scratch off any features that would normally have helped him in clear weather, starting with the monastery's outer wall. Determined soldiers with the right equipment could scale it as quickly as he had, and Bolan's only hope of spotting them would be if one or more dropped in as he was passing by their chosen spot. Trusting in God and the Sierras to protect them, the inhabitants of Holy Trinity had not installed alarms, much less surveillance cameras—which would show nothing in the whiteout, anyway.

Next, Bolan scratched the monastery's tower, standing four stories tall at the structure's northwest corner. On a sunny day or normal night, it would have made an ideal spotter's nest, allowing him to watch two sides of the roughly square property, about 270 yards to each side. That put intruders well within the range of Bolan's Steyr AUG with its Swarovski 1.5x telescopic sight, but not today, when flying snow obscured everything and high winds would wreak havoc with a bullet's flight path.

No. When the fighting started—and it *would* start, he was sure of that—it would be Bolan on the ground, alone against however many shooters U.S. Global had sent to keep one man from testifying in a court of law. As far as later prosecution went, their means and motive would be obvious, but Bolan took for granted that the shooters would not be carrying ID, much less anything connecting them to their employers. Brognola and friends, back at the DOJ, could point as many fingers as they liked, but they would have no legal grounds for new indictments if the plot worked out.

And it was nearly certain to succeed, except for one small oversight.

Instead of moving in and slaughtering their prey, along with forty-some disoriented monks, the Global team would have to reckon with the Executioner.

IT WAS A LONG, cold walk, no similarity at all to any Middle Eastern desert or the vast Australian Outback Jules Hitchener called home. He'd joined the army straight out of high school, and had trained for the Special Operations Command, winding up in the 1st Commando Regiment. Strike Swiftly was their motto, and he'd learned to do that, adding "silently and mercilessly" to the tagline during twelve months of intensive schooling.

Hitchener had passed all the courses, including cold weather ops and high altitude training in Australia's Great Dividing Range, but what he felt now was another kind of cold. It bit through insulated clothing, numbed his flesh and gnawed on his bones, a deep ache that marching failed to dissipate.

No more of this shit, he decided. From now on, sunny skies, palm trees and surf, or at the very least a hotel with a swimming pool.

That attitude had been his problem for as long as Hitchener could remember, from primary school to the day he'd gotten fed up with his company's prissy lieutenant and taken him down on a survival exercise, leaving him nude but for boots in the Tanami Desert. The only harm done was to Hitchener's career, and he'd drifted since then, like his other team members, in and out of various corporate armies until U.S. Global had snagged him on the rebound from a job in Paraguay.

Now here he was, ass deep in snow and hating it.

The money would be good, if they could pull it off, but first they needed to redeem themselves from the fiasco in New Mexico. Not my fault, Hitchener told himself, but his employer had the entire team marked in his bad books now, and there had been no argument when he'd described this cleanup job as do-or-die.

Which meant exactly what it said.

Hitchener was halfway back in the single-file column, watching his flanks while maintaining visual contact with Massimo Sordi in front of him. Losing sight of the Italian could be fatal in this weather, and being under orders not to speak would prevent him from calling out to orient himself if he got separated from the group. They all had GPS devices, but the terrain was rugged, unforgiving. If he strayed from the road, he could plummet off a cliff, and that would be the end.

Gun work was all he knew, and he was good at it. Their first attempt on this job had been foiled through no fault of their own, but now they had an easy mark—or marks, the lot of them, monks penned up in their mountain hideaway like lambs for the slaughter. Hitchener was ready to dispatch them, bank his money and move on.

Only the goddamn snow could stop him now.

THE WATSON BROTHERS were in Andrew's third-floor room, a ten-by-twelve-foot box with concrete walls and no window. Each sat at one end of the iron-framed bed, its mattress thin and sagging in the middle. Otherwise, the furniture consisted of a writing table and a wooden chair, full stop. A furnace in the basement pushed enough warm air through one floor register to keep their teeth from chattering.

Silence had stretched between them since they'd entered and sat down. Now Arthur broke the spell. "It's cold in here."

"It's winter," Andrew said. "Arthur—"

"I didn't think they'd find me here, I swear! How could they?"

"Tracking next of kin," Andrew replied.

"But you've been off the grid so long, I never thought..." He let it trail away.

"They're filthy rich, you said."

"They're filthy, period."

"That kind of money can find anyone."

"I didn't know about the marshals," Arthur said. "I listened to the news the whole way from New Mexico, but there was nothing. If I'd known..."

"What?" Andrew asked.

Arthur shrugged. "I don't know. I wouldn't have brought this mess to your doorstep."

"But it's coming now, regardless."

"Maybe not," said Arthur, hopefully.

"What do you mean? You heard—"

"Some guy I've never met before, who drops in out of nowhere dressed like a commando, telling me I need to leave with him. How do we know *he*'s not from U.S. Global?"

Andrew paused before answering. "Maybe because he didn't come in shooting?"

"But if that's an act—"

"He had the three of us—you, me, the abbot. Who'd have stopped him on his way out, after we were dead?"

Arthur could only shake his head. "I don't know. I don't know anything, these days. I should've stayed and kept my mouth shut and—"

"Secured a place in hell from knowing service to their sins?"

"It's been a long time since I thought about religion, Andy."

"I don't think about religion now, Art. I consider God's requirements for a life of contemplation and humility. It's quite a change from what I was…before."

Andy had been a singer. Not a chart-topper, but popular enough in clubs, casinos. Andrew's had been a very different life before his wife and infant daughter were obliterated by a tractor-trailer rig outside of Philadelphia thirteen years ago. After the graveside ceremony, he had disappeared. Arthur had been afraid his brother might have taken steps to join his family, until a letter had arrived from Holy Trinity announcing that he'd cleared his postulancy and become a novice with the Brothers of Saint Faustus.

That had been the first thing Arthur thought of when he felt himself about to crack as he waited to testify against his megarich employers with their ties to every filthy racket from the Middle East to South America, Johannesburg to Montreal. He had awakened in the middle of a moonless night and known nothing he told a jury under oath would stop the men in charge of U.S. Global. They were all too big to fail. They might pay fines, a tiny fraction of the loot they'd gathered over time, and they'd be back in business within months, or living out nice retirements on the Riviera, maybe on some private archipelago in the Caribbean.

And Arthur would be a hunted man until he died in

some sleazy motel room or saloon, gunned down by men who likely wouldn't even know why they were killing him.

"I'm sorry, brother," Arthur said at last. "For everything."

Andrew smiled back at him and said, "It may not be too late."

"WHERE IS HE NOW, FATHER?" asked Brother Jonathan. As prior of the monastery, he was second in command.

"Somewhere on the grounds, presumably," Brother Jerome replied. "Planning an armed defense, if we believe his story."

"That is unacceptable," said Brother Isaac, the bursar. "To shed blood on holy ground—"

"May yet be unavoidable. Again, assuming that this person spoke the truth and men are coming here to threaten us." The abbot primate's voice was resigned.

"But—"

"Brother Isaac, you know well enough our teaching as regards legitimate defense. It may have a double effect—the preservation of one's own life or another's, and the death of the aggressor. One is intended, the other is not."

A die-hard pacifist, Brother Isaac dipped his head. "But you say this man describes a team of killers coming for us, Father. We are neither armed, trained, nor prepared in any other way to deal with that, assuming he speaks the truth."

"Some of us have been trained," said Brother Jonathan. His tone was weary, almost haunted.

"With all respect," said Brother Isaac, "Vietnam was decades ago. You're not the same man now."

"You mean I'm old. That's true enough. But I remember it like yesterday, and I imagine Brother Thomas still remembers plenty from Iraq."

"Father, we should not even be considering—"

"Survival?" asked the abbot primate.

Brother Isaac stood his ground. "The Fifth Commandment forbids direct and intentional killing as gravely sinful. It also bans any action undertaken with the aim of indirectly causing death."

"I know the Ten Commandments, Brother. And *you* know our faith absolves men who are forced to kill in the performance of their lawful duty—soldiers, law enforcement officers, even state executioners."

"We still are not prepared, Father. We have no weapons, no defenses other than the outer wall, which obviously can't be trusted."

"Would you just surrender then?" asked Brother Jonathan. "Go meekly to your death, with all others beneath our roof?"

"I trust in God and prayer."

"So did many others who died in genocides, massacres, terrorist attacks..."

"Would you deny the power of faith and prayer?"

"No, Brother. But I stand by James 2:26. Faith without works is dead. And we could all be dead for no good reason, if we don't resist a clear and present evil. That's not martyrdom, it's cowardice."

"Enough!" Brother Jerome cut in. "The choice is too important to be made among us, for the others in our congregation. We shall meet and put it to a vote."

BOLAN'S WALK AROUND the monastery revealed three weak points. The wrought-iron double gate was stout enough and locked at present, but by no means impenetrable. Depending on the tools they brought along, attackers might blow it, crash it or simply fire through it while others climbed over the walls. Bolan could cover the gate, but that meant leaving at least 80 percent of the perimeter unguarded.

Weak spot number two was a wooden door set in the monastery's rear wall. It was fairly thick, much like the abbey's oversize front doors, but while secured on the inside by a hasp and chunky padlock, it would be no more difficult to take down with explosives or chainsaw than the iron front gates. And again, if Bolan watched the back door to the property, he'd leave the rest exposed.

The third point was a drain beneath the south wall, at the bottom of a gentle slope. Its heavy metal grate, removable by hand without great difficulty, barred a muddy, weed-choked tunnel roughly three feet wide and two feet deep, no longer than the wall of stone was thick. A man of normal size could wriggle through it, unobserved during the blizzard, if a watchman were not posted at the site.

Some good news: Of the three potential entry points, only the front gates could be seen on aerial surveillance photographs. The back door and the drain were invisible from overhead. Scouts could detect these security flaws given time and patience, creeping through the snowfall, following the wall outside as Bolan had already done on the inside. Depending on their numbers and degree of preparation, the attackers could strike from three points of the compass or come scrambling over walls on every side.

Last-stand heroics were not part of Bolan's normal

repertoire. He fought a fluid, mobile war whenever possible, taking the battle to his enemies, and he considered trying that tack in defense of Holy Trinity. Brother Jerome, he thought, would not object to letting him wait outside the monastery for their enemies, dealing with them as best he could beyond the abbey's hallowed grounds.

And if Bolan played that game, if he survived—then what?

The U.S. Global oligarchs, having committed to destroying the witness who could take them down, wouldn't simply shrug and wait to take their medicine in court. If they could field one group of killers, they could field another and another, keeping up the pressure until Arthur Watson either died or had a sudden change of heart. He could recant his statements to the FBI and the DOJ, although they were on record. Muddy up the waters so that reasonable doubt intruded on at least one juror's mind—perhaps assisted by a timely bribe or two—and bring about a mistrial. By the time a second trial was scheduled, anything might have happened to the state's key witness.

No. This time Bolan was fighting from the inside, certainly outnumbered, with the nature of the threat as yet to be determined. He would plan as far ahead as possible, and improvise from there.

One thing was certain: While the abbey might be holy ground, when Bolan's adversaries breached it, they'd be walking into hell.

O'CONNOR SAW THE monastery's wall loom out of nowhere in the blizzard, twelve feet tall at least, plastered with snow and ice. He raised a hand to stop the other members of his team and heard their crunching foot-steps die out as they came to a halt.

O'Connor's lungs were burning, and he knew the others must be winded, too, their muscles strained from a long slog through deep snow. His fingertips were going numb, even in his insulated gloves, and he'd already lost most of the feeling in his toes. No frost-bite there, not yet, but if they wound up laying siege to Holy Trinity, he and his men would definitely pay their pound of withered, blackened flesh.

We need a pair of eyes inside, he thought, and turned to scan the rank of faces behind him. Finally he beck-oned Killer Combs, their recon man, and waited while he shuffled forward, pushing waves of snow ahead of him with every awkward stride.

"You're going over the wall," O'Connor said. It was an order. "Alternative ways in are what we need. We'll camp at the gate, well out of sight, until you get back to me on the walkie. Clear?"

"As crystal," Combs replied. "I'll get my scaling gear laid out."

Each member of the team carried a four-pawed, collapsible grappling hook and sixty feet of Mammut 9.8 mm climbing rope, ready to ascend or rappel down any feature of the abbey, from its outer wall to its four-story tower. That was not O'Connor's favored angle of attack—he'd rather simply blow the wrought-iron gates, if there wasn't a more convenient way in—but he had planned for everything.

And once they were inside, the slaughter would begin.

O'Connor wouldn't bat an eye at killing thirty-some monks to nail one target. As it stood, his life was riding on the outcome of this second chance, along with that of every other member of his team. And if *they* died, as well, so be it. He would live to take the news back home, mission accomplished, and to claim the bounty for himself.

Rank had its privileges, and one of them was delegating death.

He saw Combs from the corner of his eye, slogging toward a corner where the south wall met the east, dragging his grappler through the snow behind him like an anchor on a boat adrift, his auto rifle slung over his shoulder. Combs was a savvy soldier and had picked a good spot to go over. There would be better traction for the hook at a corner, and he was well away from the monastery's broad front gates. O'Connor saw no reason why the monks inside should be on guard, expecting any interruption of their chants, prayers or whatever else they did during their endless days of mind-numbing routine.

Some life, he thought. At least it's almost over now.

6

Killer Combs approached the southeast corner of the monastery's looming wall with no fear that he would be spotted from the abbey's ramparts. Even though the freezing wind had slacked off slightly, he could see barely ten feet ahead and knew his all-white winter camouflage would hide him on the off chance a guard was posted somewhere outside.

He reached the twelve-foot wall, examined it for chinks and found none that would let him reach the top without assistance. That was where the grappling hook came in. Blowing the gate would be a damn sight easier, but first they had to know what waited for them inside.

Combs stepped back from the wall and swung the hook above his head, then let it fly into the storm. He lost sight of it in midflight but heard its paws clank when they hit the stony apex of the wall. Tugging the climbing line, he felt the hook give at first, sliding an inch or two, before it caught hold.

Testing the grappler's grip, he first leaned forward,

hauling on the line with everything he had, then stepped up to the wall and tried again, planting one foot and then the other against stone, letting the rope take all his weight, prepared to fall on snow and roll aside in case the hook broke free and hurtled down on top of him.

It held.

He started climbing slowly toward the goal he couldn't see. Sometimes his boots slipped a little where the stone slabs had iced over, but the rope held fast and he proceeded, insulated gloves saving his palms from being flayed. Combs reached the top sooner than he'd expected, stretched out there and rested for a moment.

The wind was picking up again, dammit. He couldn't even see what lay twelve feet below him, whether shrubbery, a lawn, pavement or some trap set to cripple him. At last, knowing the others would be waiting on him, he retrieved the climbing line and coiled it, folded up the grappling hook, then rolled off to his left and dropped into the cold white void.

BOLAN WAS ON HIS second circuit of the abbey property, looking for anything he might have missed the first time around. Nothing revealed itself, as expected, but he'd seen too many warriors die from cutting corners, letting down their guard when it mattered most of all.

Now what?

The smart move was to retreat inside for a while to thaw out, then resume his solitary sentry duty on the grounds. Otherwise, his mind could numb before his flesh gave in to the cold, leaving him vulnerable to mistakes.

Two of the monastery's major weak spots were covered now, with grenades attached to the rear gate and to the grate blocking the abbey's crude storm drain. The explosives posed no risk to any of the monastery's occupants on a day like this, but anyone who forced the gate or raised the drain's grille was in for a bone-shattering surprise. A blast at either point would also serve as an alarm, alerting Bolan to the presence of his enemies.

He wouldn't know if that would be good enough until the enemy arrived and tried to silence Arthur Watson before he could spill his guts at trial.

The worst part was that it might all turn out to be in vain.

Even if Bolan kept Watson alive and handed him back to the Feds, there was no guarantee that the runaway witness would hold up his end of the deal. He'd fled Las Cruces in a panic, and the battle that was coming would only aggravate his former employers. Watson might attempt to placate them, recant his statements to the DOJ, claim that he'd been coerced, suffered a nervous breakdown—any of a dozen legal ploys could sink his credibility and let U.S. Global off the hook.

In which case, Bolan thought, he just might visit Global himself.

But first, he had to stay alive at Holy Trinity.

As he rounded the southeast corner of the monastery, something caught his eye—an eddy in the blowing snow, a puff at ground level—and Bolan stood stock-still. Waited until a shadow rose and started moving in the direction of the abbey's tall front doors.

Bolan fell into step behind the prowler, stalking him and narrowing the gap.

"BROTHERS! REMEMBER WHO and where you are!"

Brother Jerome's stern voice, projected from the podium atop a low dais, silenced the contending voices of the abbey's other occupants. They'd gathered in the nave and listened to the abbot primate's recitation of events, starting with Brother Thomas capturing the armed intruder on their grounds, and then explaining that the invader had warned of more to follow. The monks were worried now, some of them volubly supporting a suggestion to defend the abbey, others ardently opposed. Brother Jerome was not prepared to let an argument in God's house lapse toward anarchy.

When silence was restored, he scanned each upturned face, his own wearing a mask of measured calm, and said, "I recognize the strong division of opinion on this matter, but we *will* preserve civility and brotherhood. The bickering stops now." After another sweep of the assembled audience he added, "Brother Isaac, did you have a question?"

Brother Isaac rose. "Not a question, Father, but an observation."

"Be succinct," the abbot primate advised.

"I shall." From the front row, the bursar turned to face his fellow monks, juniors and postulants. "We are not soldiers. While some of us have military backgrounds, they left that life behind to follow paths of peace through Christ's example, and vows to observe the three evangelical counsels. It is blasphemous to even speak of spilling blood on holy ground. I might add, on a private note—"

"No need for that," Brother Jerome said. "For the opposing view, a short word from our prior, Brother Jonathan."

The prior rose on cue. "As you all know, I'm one of those Brother Isaac referred to. I followed a soldier's path before I found our Savior. I take no special pride in that today, but I am not ashamed of it. Scripture grants us certain rights to self-defense. Jehovah, in the book of Exodus, is called a 'mighty man of war.' Christ himself, at the last supper, told his loyal disciples to sell their cloaks and buy swords if they were unarmed. I see it as our duty to defend the house of God and all granted asylum here."

Hushed muttering rose to the abbot primate's ears before he raised both hands to still the whispering. "You understand our options now," he said. "There is a possibility that our intruder is mistaken, or that he has attempted to deceive us. If that proves to be the case, we have one problem. If he is correct and truthful, we must face another, larger threat. In that case, the outcome, whichever path we choose, may mean the end of our community. Prepare to vote your conscience now, as guided by our Lord."

KILLER COMBS MADE a four-point landing, on toes and fingertips, cushioned by snow that puffed up in his face and blinded him. He covered for it, backing up against the wall as he unslung his Galil MAR and thumbed off its safety.

Wind whipped past him, more snow fell, but nothing else was stirring on the abbey's grounds as far as he could see. Which wasn't far at all, he granted. Three feet, max.

Recon, my ass, he thought, holding his gloved left hand at full arm's length to gauge his visibility. Beyond his fingers, the world blurred out. The abbey, more or less directly in front of him, was a hulking shadow in the blizzard, nothing more. Guards could be stationed all around it and he wouldn't see them until he was seconds short of a collision.

But why would any monks be standing sentry duty in a storm like this, freezing their holy toes off? Why would they even feel the need to mount a guard? They couldn't know that death was coming for them through the blizzard.

Could they?

No. Impossible.

The Feds might have a clue by now, after Las Cruces, if they'd done their homework on the runner. But if they were coming, Combs imagined they would have cleared the monastery out already. He wouldn't smell wood smoke rising from chimneys on the property—proof positive, in his experience, that someone was home.

He moved toward the minicastle, scanning the white landscape through tinted goggles and sweeping the muzzle of his MAR in half-circles. At intervals he stopped and turned to check his back trail, his footsteps already filling in. An army could be tailing him and Combs wouldn't have heard it with the shrill wind in his ears, but every time he checked it was the same thing: no one there.

When he reached the southeast corner of the abbey, Combs was forced to make a choice. Go west or north? He knew approximately where the front door was, had no idea where any other exits might be located. Part of his recon job was finding them, gauging how strong they were, and learning whether they were locked up tight.

Combs craned his neck to look for lighted windows in the south wall, but saw only swirling snow. It made him dizzy for a second, till he dropped his gaze

again and turned left on a whim, feeling his way along
the south wall, watching out for doors as he went. He
couldn't hear his footsteps crunching snow, but could
feel it, as if he were plodding through a field of foam
peanuts. Making all kinds of noise, he guessed, though
it would be covered by the storm.

And that's what nearly killed him.

Combs was focused on the wall beside him and
missed the *shush-shush* of footsteps closing on him
from behind. At the last second, he began to turn and
saw a shadow from the corner of his eye, before a hammer stroke numbed his right arm and sent his weapon
tumbling into knee-deep snow.

BOLAN HAD SWUNG the knife with enough force to shatter
bone, not slashing with the blade, but hammering the
intruder's right arm with a conical steel nut protruding
from the handle head. Another generation of GIs had
called that nut a skull-crusher, and it was aptly named,
well placed for cracking heads or fracturing extremities.

The man barked in pain, then stooped to grab his
fallen weapon with his left hand. Bolan aimed a kick at
his groin, but the guy wobbled in the snow and Bolan
missed his mark by inches, the steel toe of his boot
connecting with the enemy's right buttock. The man
pitched forward, sprawling. Bolan waded toward his adversary, Steyr rifle slung across his back, blade poised
to threaten, wound or kill, as circumstances might require. The other guy was quicker than he had imagined, though, and more resilient. He rolled over and
sprang to his feet.

He spun to face Bolan, half crouching in a good
defensive posture. The guy tried to reach his parka's

zipper but discovered that his right arm wasn't working properly, so he brought the left around to cover for its injured mate. Seizing the moment, Bolan threw a straight jab at the guy's mask and goggles, the cast-bronze knuckles on his trench knife's grip causing extra damage.

The prowler staggered back from the crunching impact, left arm flailing for balance, while a crimson floral pattern blossomed on the white mask, where his nose should be.

And once again, the guy recovered without falling. Snorting bloody bubbles through his mask, he somehow reached a hidden pistol with his left hand, drew it, and was raising it toward Bolan's chest when Bolan slashed the guy's forearm through the parka's padded sleeve. Blood stained the snow, then the prowler's sidearm fell on top of it and punched a hole through sullied powder toward the hidden ground beneath.

The interloper snarled and came at Bolan, both arms raised, one trailing vermilion fringe, the other flopping strangely. The soldier met him with a rising thrust below the sternum, six-plus inches of his blade piercing the parka, abdomen and diaphragm, slicing through the aortal wall.

The intruder dropped to his knees at Bolan's feet, then toppled over backward, shuddering, but not from cold. His feet kicked lazily in the snow, then stopped moving altogether. Bolan had hoped to grill this man about his comrades, their firepower, but he'd had no choice. One of them had to die.

The Executioner peeled the ski mask back and stared into a face like countless others, all-American, blanched by cold and blood loss so that scattered freckles stood in stark relief across the flattened nose.

Somebody's brother, someone's son. But the man had chosen to become a killer, and that choice had sealed his fate.

Bolan sheathed his blade and pulled the mask back into place before he stooped to move the corpse.

THE VOTE WAS TIED, seventeen to seventeen, with postulants abstaining. Brother Jerome had the authority to break the tie, if he so chose. For some minor controversy, like the decision to plant kale or lettuce in the spring, or the menu for a high feast day, perhaps, he might have left the brothers to debate and settle it among themselves, but this was different.

This vote could mean life or death.

On Brother Isaac's side, the pacifists contended that a prayerful mien might spare them from annihilation, or at least send them to meet their Savior with clean hands and souls. Those backing Brother Jonathan, conversely, thought it was their Christian duty to resist evil with all their might in God's house, to prevent defilement of the abbey.

Caught between the two, Brother Jerome was not convinced by either course of action.

Thirty-six pairs of eyes focused on him as he loomed above them at the pulpit. The brothers were expectant, uneasy. They were on the verge of losing everything, their lives included, and while some would trust his judgment, Jerome knew others might break discipline if he did not decide the vote their way. And what recourse would be left to him in that event?

What punishment could he impose that would impress brothers about to die?

"Before I cast my vote," Brother Jerome began, "I want you all to know that I have listened to both sides and understand the arguments in all sincerity. Both sides advance positions founded in scripture and the teachings of the church. Neither is wrong per se. But a matter of this gravity demands a solution, and the force of God Himself outside these walls prevents us from consulting the archdiocese. Therefore, I must decide, and I ask each member of the congregation to abide by my decision to the best of his ability."

The nave was deathly silent, no more murmuring, each monk rooted to his pew. Scanning the audience, Brother Jerome saw Brother Andrew and his sibling seated side by side, the postulant pale-faced, as if his execution was the subject of their vote. In a way, it was. Defending Holy Trinity against its worldly enemies meant defending Arthur, however hopeless that might be. Silent acceptance of whatever lay in store could easily be seen as an abandonment of their most recent postulant.

The worst of it, Brother Jerome thought, was that either way he cast his vote, the end result would likely be identical. "Brothers," he began.

And then the doors burst open, and Matthew Cooper strode into the room.

"They're here."

7

"He should be back by now," said Colin Hume. "It's been twenty minutes."

"He had lots of ground to cover," O'Connor answered.

"Not *that* much," Ismael Ornelas countered.

Gilad Cohen added, "He has a radio."

And they were right, of course. Even with close to zero visibility, Combs should have made a once-around and come back to report by this time—unless he'd run into some kind of opposition.

Such as what? O'Connor asked himself, and couldn't come up with an explanation he liked.

The place looked like a fortress, but it was a *monastery*. Filled with monks, for God's sake. They were not soldiers, and they sure as hell weren't on a par with Killer Combs or any other members of O'Connor's crew.

He let another five minutes slip by, then said, "All right, that's long enough."

"We going in?" Tyrone Jackson asked. "Or you gonna call 'em out?"

Another question O'Connor had to answer for himself. He'd brought an ultracompact ThunderPower megaphone along, just in case someone inside the abbey wanted to negotiate. If he could avoid direct assault over the walls, O'Connor would be good with that. Feed the monks some promises, convince them to send out their visitor, then mop up all the witnesses when he was dead. With any luck, no one would find their bodies until spring.

But if they'd captured Combs, unlikely as it seemed, that altered everything.

Barring surrender of their primary target, O'Connor's aim was infiltration, taking the monks by surprise while they were at the gates, distracted, and eliminate them.

Easy. But he'd had one soldier go astray already, vanishing into the freezing air.

"Before we jump, I need two men to scout the wall," O'Connor said. "Hitchener, you go around the east side. Goonie, take the west. Watch out for any points of entry. When you meet up, come back and report."

"No worries," Goonie Gounden said.

"On it," Hitchener replied.

Then they were gone, two shadows fading into white. The storm seemed to be growing more intense. An east wind pressed O'Connor's parka tight against the right side of his body, tried to push him over. He stood against it, feet planted a yard apart, and wondered when he'd ever felt as miserable.

Call it ten minutes, maybe fifteen tops, before his second team of scouts returned and briefed him on the monastery's weaknesses. When he'd received that information, he'd decide whether to make the pitch he'd planned in transit from New Mexico, or simply take the place by storm.

A firestorm in a snowstorm.

That was almost good enough to make him smile behind his ski mask.

Almost.

"You killed him?" There was something close to horror in the abbot primate's voice, leavened with sorrow.

"There was no choice," Bolan said. "They sent him in to scout the place, report back, tell them where and how to breach the wall. He had a gun."

"And who is 'they'?" Brother Jerome inquired.

"You want names," Bolan said, "I can't help you. I can tell you they're well-armed—" he offered up the Galil MAR as proof "—and they aren't playing games. I got lucky this time, but they're out there, no question."

"But what if you're wrong?" Brother Isaac chimed in.

"This didn't fall out of the sky," Bolan replied, placing the captured rifle on the lectern.

"I mean," Brother Isaac went on, "what if this prowler was alone? You came to us without assistance. Might he not have done the same?"

Bolan shook his head. "We know at least four shooters hit the marshals in Las Cruces. For a place like this, they'd pull out all the stops."

"But—"

"That's enough," Brother Jerome cut off the argument and turned back to Bolan. "How many others would you estimate, in your professional opinion?"

"Given their resources, I'd peg ten as the minimum to penetrate and occupy a place this size. With the deep pockets funding them, it could be double that. We have no way of knowing till they hit us."

"Us?" Brother Isaac interjected. "May I remind you that they only want the postulant, who by his own admission is a criminal?"

"You'd give him up?" asked Brother Jonathan, his gruff voice stony cold.

"It wouldn't matter," Bolan said. "I've told you once already that they don't leave witnesses."

"But we aren't witnesses!" said Brother Isaac. "No one here has seen them yet, except for you. They could remove their friend's remains and go."

Isaac was living in a dream world spun from fear. "You think they'll trust you to forget about all this and not report it to authorities?" Bolan asked. "Why? Because you give your solemn word?"

"We don't *know* anything!"

"I know this," said the abbot primate. "Sanctuary is an ancient sacred principle. We would not hand the postulant to forces of the state, and I will not sanction delivering him to a gang of murderers outside our gates."

"And what is the alternative, Father?" Brother Isaac's face had grown red.

"Resistance to the limits of our personal abilities. I cast my vote, reluctantly, with Brother Jonathan."

The gathered monks began to murmur in reaction to the abbot's decision.

Saddened by victory, the prior reached past Bolan, picked up the MAR and briefly studied it. "These weren't around when I was in the service, but I can see it's borrowed from the AK-47 on its gas diversion system." Glancing up at Bolan, he concluded, "Funny how it never really goes away."

"Two rifles against twenty," Brother Isaac added, almost scornfully.

"That's twenty at the top end," Bolan said. "We could get half of that, maybe a dozen."

"Betting with our lives." A bitter note was edging fear out of the bursar's voice.

"We'll pick up other weapons as we go along," Bolan replied.

"Or else you'll die and take us with you." Brother Isaac turned away.

"Do not forget your place," Brother Jerome said sternly, as the bursar left the nave. "Or your duty."

Washington, D.C.

"STILL NOTHING?" HAL BROGNOLA asked Barbara Price over the phone.

"They're socked in with the storm out there. No satellite connection at the moment, period."

"I was afraid of that," Brognola said. "Keep checking, will you, and get back to me."

"Of course."

The California blizzard was expected to continue in the High Sierras for another day, at least, and maybe through the weekend. There was nothing anyone could do about it but complain, or send a prayer aloft if they were so inclined.

Brognola wondered if the monks at Holy Trinity were praying now, and what they might be asking for. Salvation? Maybe just the strength to live another day?

Or were they dead and gone already?

Brognola didn't like being out of touch with Bolan on a job like this. The standing rule with the soldier on a mission was short and sweet: Do Not Disturb. That said, Bolan usually checked in with sit reps, and the Farm could generally ping his sat phone to locate him. With the stakes so high, being out of the loop made Brognola uneasy.

He had already spoken twice to Jack Grimaldi in Modesto. Nothing there, and Brognola didn't intend to call again unless he had new information. The pilot would be heading back out into the storm soon for his rendezvous with Bolan, and Brognola expected to get an update then.

Relax, he told himself. And knew it was impossible.

Holy Trinity Monastery

SPIKE O'CONNOR CHECKED his watch again, restless and trying to hide it for his men's sake and his own. He'd never drawn a mission quite like this, but he knew one thing for certain: no one benefited from a leader who was jumpy and about to lose it.

"They've still got some time." Ornelas spoke up at his elbow, emphasizing Spike's concern.

"I know it," he replied without elaboration.

"I'm just sayin'."

"Yeah, well, don't."

Gerald O'Connor was a former Navy SEAL, thirty years old. He'd missed the gig to smoke bin Laden by a stroke of luck that still made him resentful. Team Six got the assignment instead of his unit; now they had ghostwritten books on the bestseller list and a made-for-TV movie showing everyone what fantastic heroes they were. O'Connor wasn't envious, exactly, but—screw that. Of course he was. He could have been a millionaire, relaxing on an island somewhere with a couple of bikini babes right now, instead of standing ass-deep in a snowbank waiting for a chance to kill a bunch of monks and some guy nobody had ever heard of .

Not that he minded killing. That was part of why he'd joined the service and endured the brutal training necessary to become a SEAL. He wanted *action,* not an endless cruise around the world with nothing at the end but some tattoos to show for it. America had been at war since he was in middle school, and O'Connor felt that he was missing out. Places to go, people to kill.

He had been on some missions that would probably be classified until the end of time, but ultimately, he'd rebelled against the discipline, like most of the ex-soldiers who comprised his present team. They were misfits, good for only one thing in this world: destruction.

"I see 'em," said Ornelas, pointing through the ever-shifting veil of snow.

O'Connor squinted through his goggles, leaning forward slightly, then he had it. Two hunched shadows approaching, clad in white and clutching weapons to their chests.

He waited for the scouts to reach him, standing easy. "Well?" he asked when they were close.

Goonie spoke first. It was a lousy nickname, but with Gounden for a last name, what could you expect? "They've got a storm drain near the northwest corner, covered by a grate. It's wide enough to pass through and the grate isn't cemented down."

"Okay."

"And there's a door around back," said Hitchener.

"Middle of the west wall. Made of wood, not like the front gates."

"Did you try it?" O'Connor asked.

"You didn't authorize a penetration," the Aussie replied,

Fair enough. He'd split the team, three men to take the west gate, three more on the drain, and four with him out front to storm the main gate if, as he expected, Spike couldn't convince the abbey's holy Joes to give up their visitor. Surrender would make things easier, but Spike had nothing against doing it the hard way.

Truth be told, that was his preference.

"IT'S A GALIL," said Brother Thomas. "Made by IMI—Israel Military Industries. I never trained on one this small when I was in the Corps, but yeah, there's no mistaking it."

"They weren't around in my day," Brother Jonathan added.

"It's 5.56 mm," Brother Thomas told him, "but I guess you saw that. Spits the casings out somewhere around 650 rounds per minute. Dents a lot of them, which makes it lousy for reloading, but it does the job. Funny the way it all comes back so quick. Is it like that for you?"

"Yeah, funny," Brother Jonathan said, not smiling.

"Hey, I didn't mean—"

"This guy you ran into, did he have any extra magazines?" the prior asked Bolan.

"Half a dozen in a bandoleer," Bolan replied. "I left them downstairs, by the front door."

"So we've got two weapons now," Brother Thomas

observed. "That's nowhere near enough to guard a place this size."

He was right. Two rifles wouldn't cut it, even on a clear day, with the Steyr's maximum effective range topped out around three hundred yards, and less for the stubby Galil. If the enemy rushed them in sufficient numbers, spread out along the perimeter, the abbey would be overrun. That meant fighting in the building itself, unless they were able to keep the invaders outside.

How many doors and windows granted access to the abbey proper? How many monks would be willing to raise a hand in self-defense?

He asked the latter question, though a bit more tactfully. The two brothers with military service in their backgrounds locked eyes for a heartbeat.

"Seventeen, counting us two. The vote was a tie without Brother Jerome," Brother Jonathan said.

"Will he fight?" Bolan asked.

"Hard to say," Brother Thomas replied. "He's not trained, anyhow."

"Nor is anyone else," Brother Jonathan said.

"We don't have time to train them," Bolan granted, "and we only have four guns." He'd given Brother Thomas the dead scout's Glock and its spare magazines, keeping the Beretta 93R for himself. "The rest will have to use whatever's handy from the kitchen, garden tools—"

"They're outside, in a shed," said Brother Jonathan. "Four spades, four rakes, four hoes. Two trowels, I think. One garden claw."

"The kitchen's got a load of knives, all sizes, plenty for the seventeen," Brother Thomas added.

Which meant close quarters combat only, going

hand-to-hand against trained adversaries packing automatic rifles and whatever else they'd brought to the party. Handguns, almost certainly for backup, maybe shotguns and a sniper's piece or two.

"Pretty grim," said the prior. "We might be able to delay them on the windows."

Pretty grim indeed, Bolan thought. His task was no longer as simple as protecting a witness and securing the monastery.

Now, he'd be doing everything in his power to prevent a massacre.

"ARE THE C-4 charges ready?" Spike O'Connor asked their demo man.

"Two for the gates, but one should be enough," Kurt Mueller answered. He was ex-Kommando Spezialkräfte, or KSK, part of Germany's crack Special Operations Division.

"Better safe than sorry," said O'Connor. "Hook 'em up before I try to talk the padres out of there."

"They won't surrender," Ornelas said. He was Mexican, raised Catholic, and knew his priests. He was also formerly a sergeant with the Cuerpo de Fuerzas Especiales de México, Mexican Special Forces, cut from the ranks in a shake-up involving collusion with one of the country's top drug cartels.

"It doesn't matter," said O'Connor. "Everybody goes, regardless."

"I'm just saying, it's a waste of time negotiating."

"Noted. You, Denikin and Cohen take the west gate. Keep your walkies on. Be ready for my signal."

"Signal, right." Ornelas turned away to fetch the others Spike had named.

When he was gone, O'Connor told Hitchener, "You're on the storm drain with Goonie and Hume."

"Roger that."

O'Connor was keeping the rest: Mueller to blow the gates, Blake and Jackson with their sniper rifles, and Sordi, the Italian, with his Benelli Super 90 shotgun. Sordi was a veteran of Italy's 9th Parachute Assault Regiment, tested by fire in Libya and Afghanistan. Wine was his special vice, but he was sober as a judge today.

Most judges, anyhow.

O'Connor had the ThunderPower megaphone in hand, his short speech memorized. The abbey's occupants had one chance to surrender Arthur Watson, and if they refused—as he fully expected—he would blow the gates, signal the other entry teams via his walkie-talkie, and the wholesale slaughter would begin. Five minutes was nothing in the universal scheme of things.

Only one detail had Spike O'Connor's nerves on edge. What had become of Killer Combs?

It wasn't just the loss of one man that concerned him. Combs was packing a Galil MAR carbine, which meant whoever took him out must have it now. One of the monks? Someone else? If there were Feds beyond the wall, they would have shown themselves by now instead of lying back in ambush.

Call it one man with a modern weapon then, the others picking up whatever came to hand for cutting, clubbing, breaking bones. Even outnumbered three or four to one, O'Connor liked the odds.

The white day would be turning red before much longer, and the future would be green when they received their payoff for a job well done, if flubbed at the beginning. Only final resolutions counted in the killing game, and there was no way in the world O'Connor's team could lose.

No way at all.

8

Bolan was standing on the abbey's porch, the front gates veiled by writhing sheets of snow, when a voice reached his ears. He guessed the megaphone was cranked up to full power, but the message still had trouble competing with the howling wind. He picked up most of it and managed to fill in the rest from context. They wanted Watson, they said, and if the monks handed him over, they'd leave in peace. Yeah, right.

He pictured the attackers, all dressed like the scout he'd already eliminated. They'd be armed about the same way, maybe variations in the choice of automatic weapons, but they had a clear superiority on firepower. The dead man had been packing half a dozen extra magazines for his Galil. Take that as standard and extrapolate for nine guns minimum: 2,200 rounds to burn, plus sidearms and their spare mags, possibly grenades.

All that against his own gear: 330 rounds for the Steyr, one hundred for the Beretta, and two M26 grenades besides the pair he'd set as booby traps for infiltrators. Brother Jonathan had 245 rounds for his captured Galil MAR, and Brother Thomas had forty-five rounds for the Glock 23. Bolan considered the remaining fifteen monks who'd voted to defend the abbey with their motley arsenal of knives, hammers and garden tools, then put them out of mind. They were a last line of defense on doors and windows, nothing more.

No matter how he stacked it, the home team would be outnumbered and outgunned.

The storm was neutral. It would blind both sides equally, slowing their movements and reaction times, effectively preventing any long-range sniping that might have stacked the killer odds even more heavily against the abbey's occupants. Bolan took for granted that the men outside the walls had no more knowledge of the abbey's grounds than he'd had when he arrived, likely working from the same satellite photos he had reviewed.

Counting the minutes in his head, Bolan decided he had ninety seconds left, approximately, before something happened. What that *something* might turn out to be, he couldn't say: grenades over the wall, an RPG to clear the wrought-iron gates, white figures scrambling over on all sides. Whatever form the blitz assumed, he had to hope they would be ready for it.

Brother Jonathan was stationed at the southwest corner of the abbey, in a recessed doorway, bundled up as best he could be for the cold, masked by a homemade scarf under his cowl. Brother Thomas had northeast watch, hunkered inside a kind of concrete foxhole excavated for a basement window, eyes around knee level for a passing enemy.

Not a great defense, but Bolan had seen worse. He had survived worse—which, of course, meant nothing in the present situation. No man entered combat with a guarantee of coming out the other side alive, intact.

His mental clock was still four seconds short of a five full minutes when the front gates blew, a flash of fire followed by a thunderclap that punched a brief hole in the storm and let him see one of the tall gates swinging inward, while its mate sagged to the right, top hinges severed from the wall.

Darting figures rushed the gates, and the snow closed in again, concealing them as they made their way into the monastery.

THE BLAST, THOUGH SLIGHTLY muted by the blizzard, rocked O'Connor where he stood with his strike team, well back from Ground Zero.

As the shock waves and echoes faded, he told the others, "Split up once we get inside. Remember, no one lives, but Arthur Watson is the money shot. You all have photos of the target. Radio a heads-up if you bag him."

No one bothered answering. They'd heard it all before.

"Move out!" he snapped, and led the way, jogging as best he could through snow that was rising quickly toward hip level.

Mueller met him at the twisted, smoking gates, where heat from the explosion had reduced the snow to runny slush.

O'Connor nodded to the German, all the thanks Mueller would get for being competent. Stepping through the gates, they encountered a chest-high wall of snow, piled up in the force of the blast. Swinging the butt of his Galil as if it were a dull machete hacking jungle ferns, O'Connor blazed a slow trail toward the abbey's central structure, still a hulking shadow in the storm.

No opposition yet, but he hadn't expected any. The monks might stage some kind of martyrs' stand inside the building—bar the doors and man the windows, armed with knives, screwdrivers, hammers if they had the guts for it—but they couldn't hold out for long against a well-armed entry team. The trick, inside a place this big, would be ensuring they left no one alive, huddled inside a closet or some kind of hidden passageway. Who could predict how restless monks had tunneled through the place, with nothing else to do but sit and pray?

The abbey's wide stone porch was about fifty yards from the front gate. O'Connor had covered about a third of that distance, with the others fanning out around him, when he was stopped short by the echo of a second, smaller detonation on the grounds. He couldn't place it accurately with the storm screaming around him, but it seemed to come from somewhere on his right, toward the north wall.

The storm drain?

No. It couldn't be. Aside from Mueller, no one on his team was carrying explosives, and the blast had not been loud enough for a C-4, anyway. More like a hand grenade, but that was totally crazy. The idea of a grenade inside a monastery was absurd. Where would it come from? Who among the monks would even understand its firing mechanism?

Perhaps a small propane tank, then. But what would have set it off? There'd been no gunfire yet, no sounds of battle on the abbey grounds at all.

Forget about it. He would let the others deal with it, whatever *it* was, while he concentrated on their goal.

JULES HITCHENER AND his two companions at the north wall heard the abbey's gates blow. There was no mistaking that sound, for a combat veteran or anyone who'd worked around explosives in civilian life. It was C-4, delivering a heavy knockout punch: their signal to proceed.

"Okay, let's do it," Hitchener said.

Goonie was on his knees already, having cleared the snow that clogged the abbey's storm drain, opening a tunnel wide enough for them to crawl through one by one after he shoved the inner grate aside. On Hitchener's order, Goonie went belly-down and started wriggling underneath the stone wall, a strange sight as his head and shoulders vanished, followed by his torso, leaving only arse and legs protruding.

"Almost got it here." His muffled voice came back to Hitchener and the former SAS man, Colin Hume, who stood to his left. "It's sticking, but—"

Then the world exploded in their faces.

The blast pitched the headless, armless remnants of Goonie Gounden back toward his two cohorts, spewing blood and bits of flesh from the storm drain onto white jumpsuits and boots. Hitchener lurched backward, lost his footing in the muck and went down on his backside, one of Gounden's boots jammed underneath him. He rolled away from it and came up kneeling, finger tight around the trigger of his MAR, but no targets appeared before him.

Hume was sputtering and cursing, swiping gore from his goggles and ski mask. He had been stooping slightly when the blast went off, watching Goonie's progress through the drain, and so had taken part of their truncated comrade in the face.

"What was that?" the Brit demanded. "I mean, what in bloody hell was *that?*"

"A trap," Hitchener replied, stating the obvious. "Maybe some kind of IED."

"A bloody IED? What kind of monks are these we're up against here?"

"It makes no difference. The way's clear now."

Hume turned his bloody mask toward Hitchener. "What? You don't know that."

"How many bombs do you suppose they'd put on one storm drain?"

"But they'll have heard it. They'll be coming out with axes or whatever else they've got in there."

"Sod off then," Hitchener sneered. "I'm going in."

Before Hume could reply, Hitchener grabbed Gounden's left ankle and began to haul the shattered corpse away. Hume pitched in, clearing the drain that had become a gory opening on God knew what.

That task accomplished, Hitchener bellied down and pushed off with his toes, arms out ahead of him, clutching his Galil and prepared to fire at any sign of opposition on the other side, assuming that he had the chance. Goonie had cleared the grate, he saw, as he wriggled through blood and brains and lumpy entrails, toward the clean white snow beyond the blast zone.

Hitchener braced himself for anything—a blade hacking his arms, a bludgeon to the skull—but nothing happened. Seconds after shoving into it, he cleared the tunnel and scrambled to his feet once more. Behind him, grunting curses as he came, Hume followed through the chute.

THE FIRST EXPLOSION startled Brother Jonathan, although he'd been expecting something. In ordinary circumstances, he would have responded to the blast by rushing toward the sound to see if any of his brothers had been injured or the abbey damaged. But in these most extraordinary circumstances, he obeyed the orders Matthew Cooper had delivered when they separated, and stood fast in his position at the monastery's southwest corner.

It was bitterly cold out, well below zero, but the tremors he felt now came from fear and raw excitement, the same mixture of emotions he'd experienced during long-range patrols in Vietnam so many years ago, stalking an enemy who could be anyone and anywhere. Each time he'd left base camp had felt like a death wish. He'd half expected ambush, booby traps, a snakebite, even "friendly" fire at every turn. Not that the camp itself was ever safe from mortar rounds, snipers or RPGs fired in the middle of the sweaty, sleepless night.

He'd hated Nam while he was there—or so he'd told himself. Battling post-traumatic stress disorder in the years that followed took him from the self-induced oblivion of drugs and liquor to the isolated mountain fortress where he stood now, pledged to service of the Lord, but trembling with the same sensations he had felt back then, during his time in hell.

And recognizing, to his own astonishment, that it was not all bad.

A part of him had relished hunting humans in the jungle, coming back after a skirmish to inflate his own accomplishments, sometimes transforming a clutch of peasants killed by accident into a wily band of enemies. The weapon in his hands reminded Brother Jonathan that God was not the only one with power over life and death.

He waited, while his conflicting urges, fight or flight, grappled for primacy. Military training and more recently acquired meditation skills enabled Brother Jonathan to stand his frozen ground, trusting Matt Cooper to repel invaders at the abbey's gates, while he stood watch behind.

The second, smaller blast was no surprise. Cooper had briefed him on the traps he'd set with frag grenades to stop intruders on their flanks. This one, judging from its distance and direction, had been the storm drain underneath the north wall of the monastery. Someone had tried to move the grating there and had paid a price for it. But a grenade would not have brought the wall down, so the way would still be open if invaders had the nerve to crawl through human wreckage.

Not my post, he told himself. Covering that end of the abbey fell to Brother Thomas in his basement window pit, half-filled with freezing snow. Instinct urged Brother Jonathan to go and help him, but he swallowed it, a jagged, bitter pill.

And when the third blast came, much closer, from the rear gate, he was ready. Stepping out into the storm with his Galil, imagining a steaming rain forest instead of a blizzard, he moved to meet the unknown enemy.

"IT'S LOCKED," Gilad Cohen announced.

"No shit," Ismael Ornelas said. "You think they'd leave it open for us?"

"No problem," said the former Spetsnaz soldier, Denikin. Ornelas watched him remove a suppressed SIG Sauer P226 from his parka. Stepping past his comrades,

Denikin aimed at the point where it appeared a hasp and lock were bolted to the other side. "Fire in the hole!" he said, and pumped four muffled rounds through aged wood, blowing the gate's padlock away.

O'Connor had already blown the front gates, right on time, and Denikin's last shot touched off another blast, making the trio flinch and duck until they realized it wasn't close at hand. The echo came from somewhere to their left.

"The drain," said Cohen.

"They weren't 'sposed to blow it out," Ornelas said.

"They didn't," the Israeli answered. "None of us are packing charges, are we?"

Ornelas could almost see Denikin grinning through his ski mask. "So the drain blew them," he said. "Crafty, these monks, eh?"

Cohen cursed. "Why would they have explosives?"

"We can ask them," said Ornelas, "when we get inside."

Denikin stepped back from the bullet-punctured gate. "After you."

"If it was wired, it should have detonated from the gunfire, right?" Cohen asked.

"Jesus," Ornelas sneered as he brushed past them. "I'll go first if you are both cowards."

There was no knob on the outside of the gate. Ornelas pushed it cautiously, but it was wedged against a three-foot mound of snow inside. He had to put his back into it, straining, to produce the smallest movement.

"Shit! Help me, will you?"

Denikin and Cohen both came forward, putting shoulders to the gate, boots sliding in the snow as they shoved together. It was moving now, still slowly, but surrendering to their determination. Just another foot or so, Ornelas thought, and he could slip through to the other side, clear out some of the snow and pull.

He was startled when his feet slid out from under him. He dropped to his knees, head partway through the open gate. He caught a fleeting glimpse of something round, dull green, metallic, as it dropped into the snow and out of sight, perhaps two feet in front of him.

"Grenade!" Ornelas shouted, throwing himself backward and scrambling onto his knees in the seconds that remained to him before the world went white and the concussion of a close-range detonation deafened him.

Hot shrapnel stung his buttocks through the insulated jumpsuit, more slapping against his heavy boot soles as he lay facedown, feet toward the source of the explosion. Once he'd judged the pain, deciding that it likely wasn't lethal, he remembered that the deadly chaff from a grenade blast normally flew up and out, sparing prone bodies on occasion, more or less.

The question now: was Ornelas more or less wounded?

And were his comrades still alive?

He rolled onto his back, grimacing through his ski mask, and was instantly rewarded as the cold snow soothed his stinging wounds. When he slid a glove beneath his upper thigh it came back splotched with blood, but not as much as he'd expected. It would be painful to stand and walk, but there would be no gusher from a severed artery to bring him down, only flesh wounds that hurt like hell.

Cohen was on his knees, as if he were a pilgrim praying at the abbey's gate. When Ornelas called to him, he turned slowly, shuffling around, to show a ski mask crimson on the left side, the left lens of his goggles scarred.

"You blind?" Ornelas asked him, his voice muffled by the ringing in his ears.

"Fuck you," the Israeli said, as if that answered everything.

Aleksei Denikin was on his feet, barely, leaning against the stone wall. One of his sleeves was torn and gaping open, bloodied, but he used both hands to clutch his rifle. "I can fight," he said.

Ornelas struggled to his feet, retrieving his Benelli shotgun from the snow, and turned back to the gate. "Okay," he said to both of them. "Let's show these *cabrones* who they're messing with."

BOLAN WAS ALREADY in motion when the two grenades exploded, their detonations separated by seconds. He hoped that both had done their job, disabling some of his adversaries if they weren't killed outright. It was probably too much to count on more than one death at each entry point, but he would take whatever he could get, leaving the Brothers Jonathan and Thomas to mop up as best they could.

The mission wasn't going as he'd planned, but what job ever did? Combat was fluid, turbulent, with nothing guaranteed except the unexpected. Anything could happen, and it usually did. Toss in a blizzard for variety, and battle plans were literally written on the wind.

Bolan had lost the shadow shapes almost as soon as they appeared before him, slipping past the abbey's violated gates. He was sure of three at least. Behind them had been other shadows, but he couldn't tell if those were soldiers on the move or optical illusions cast up by the storm.

Advancing through the drifts, Bolan scanned to his right and left, trying to calculate how far his enemies could have traveled with the same wind in their faces, same snow making every step a slogging ordeal. Bolan's legs were burning, overworked and undernourished as the cold slowed his circulation. He wasn't freezing yet, but in a game where every microsecond counted, delayed response time could be fatal.

Death did not intimidate the Executioner. He'd seen and dealt out far too much of it to quail before the final mystery. But he didn't intend to fall with his mission incomplete, abandoning the witness he had come to rescue, and the other occupants of Holy Trinity, to a pack of human wolves.

In front of him, a shadow moved behind a rippling screen of snow. Bolan stopped short, lifted the Steyr to his shoulder and took aim.

9

U.S. Global Finance Headquarters, Manhattan

"Remind me why we keep you on the payroll," Sheldon Page demanded. He was stone-faced, no names spoken, always a bad sign.

"Because I get things done," Brad Kemper said, determined not to sweat before his three inquisitors.

"Correction," Cornell Dubois said. "You *got* things done, past tense, on other jobs. All you've accomplished this time, when we need you most, is stirring up a hornet's nest."

"Three U.S. marshals dead," Reginald Manson interjected, "and our witness in the wind. A lot of bullshit promises."

"I've told you where he is," Kemper replied to all of them at once. "My people have him pinned down where escape, in my view, is impossible."

"In your view," Page replied, keeping the tag-team effort going. "If that's true, why is the bastard still alive?"

"He may be dead by now." It sounded lame, but Kemper put a brave face on it, still not trembling visibly. He'd seen the guards outside, ostensibly his men, but in reality owned by the company. He wondered if he'd leave the plushly furnished meeting room alive.

"*May* be?" The echo came from Manson, switching up the order of attack now. "You can't even tell us that?"

"What I've *already* told you is they've got a blizzard in the mountains where he's hiding, breaking all the records for this time of year. Communications are—"

"Spare us the Weather Channel reruns." Dubois sneered. "You've spent the best part of a million dollars on the hunt so far, and now you're blaming acts of God for failure? That's pathetic."

Kemper felt the color rising in his cheeks, knew anger was his enemy right now, but couldn't altogether rein it in. A million bucks was chump change to these bloated ticks, and they were blaming *him* because it snowed in California?

"A million or a billion," he replied, keeping his tone in check. "You can't buy off the weather. No one in the area has cell reception, rich or poor. Surveillance satellites see nothing but the clouds and snow downstairs. I know my men are working on it, and they may be done by now, but a report will have to wait until the weather clears or they clear out. That's all there is to it."

"In which case," Page observed, "we really don't need you at all, do we? Based on your own words, *our* men will call in their report sooner or later, one way or another. You appear to be superfluous, *n'est-ce pas?*"

Kemper despised rich people who affected foreign phrases in a futile bid to sound more cultured than they were, but this one—these three—signed his hefty pay-

checks, and right now, they controlled whether he lived
to see another day.

So, what to do? When he was in a high-stakes poker
game and holding shit, he nearly always bluffed. The
only difference: today his head was in the pot.

He shrugged, trying to keep it casual, and said, "You
want to take me off the board, that's your prerogative. I
reckon I could only kill one of you, maybe scar another
up for life, before you hit the panic button and the boys
outside finish your dirty work."

It pleased him to observe the sudden fading of their
sunlamp tans.

Page growled, "No, listen here—"

"Or," Kemper interrupted him, "we could be reasonable men and wait until the call comes through. If
you're dissatisfied with the report, lay down some tarp,
hand me a sidearm loaded with a single round. I'll finish it myself, right here."

The masters of his fate exchanged glances, a silent
message passing between them. Finally, as president,
Page handed down the verdict.

"We'll wait," he said, "but not much longer. In the
meantime, you'll remain here as our guest."

Kemper allowed himself a small smile. "Works for
me."

Holy Trinity Monastery

BOLAN, HALF-BLINDED by the storm, switched his Steyr
AUG to semiauto fire, intending to save on ammunition in the crunch and limit his exposure to return fire
targeting his muzzle flashes.

But so far, it wasn't working out.

His first target had seemed substantial as he lightly stroked the bullpup's trigger, but the shadow vanished as his bullet left the muzzle, drilling through the snow. Bolan couldn't say if the prowler had stumbled and fallen or ducked to one side. He was there and then gone, and the first shot was wasted.

Worse yet, the burst set three Galils yapping at Bolan, their 5.56 mm chatter punctuated by two booming shotgun blasts. He hit the deck—in this case, the powder—and heard projectiles snapping overhead while the storm moaned.

Bolan lay waiting for the hunters to try again. Fire discipline was critical in close range combat, but even the best teams in the world often had one guy who got antsy, hyped up by the smell of burning gunpowder. This group was no exception. When another short Galil burst came at Bolan from his right, he aimed a double-tap above his muzzle flash, then rolled aside before the others started tearing up his snow nest, raising foot-high geysers that were instantly dispersed by howling wind.

Bolan missed the second wave of muzzle flashes as he tumbled out of line, but far from out of range. Next time he fired, if stray rounds didn't find him first, the hunters would return more grazing fire, and it was likely they'd be closer.

Marking where his enemies had been last time they fired en masse, with no idea how far they'd moved since then, Bolan unclipped his next-to-last M26 grenade and pulled the safety pin, released the spoon and counted off two seconds before he lobbed it overhand, as high as he could loft it, hoping for an airburst. When it blew, spraying shrapnel over a rough fifteen-yard radius, he might have heard a scream, but couldn't tell for sure with so much competition from the storm.

Modesto City–County Airport

WHEN THE SAT phone buzzed, Grimaldi flinched, slopping hot coffee on his hand. He cursed and answered the phone.

"Jack here."

Hal Brognola's voice came back at him. "No news, I take it?"

"Nada. The storm has basically wiped out reception."

"Yeah, I was afraid of that. We're blind here, too, as far as any bird's-eye views."

Not knowing was the worst. Dropping a soldier—hell, a friend—into the viper's den was bad enough, but losing track of him, with no way of telling whether he was still alive or not, was worse. For this job, Bolan had been fitted with a Pocketfinder GPS locator, in addition to the chip inside his sat phone. If he got separated from his phone during the jump, hiking through the High Sierras or fighting for his life, the backup device could locate Bolan in a pinch, alive or otherwise. But in weather this bad, both tracking methods were moot. Which was why they'd agreed on a rendezvous near the monastery. If Bolan wasn't there to meet the Cessna…well, Grimaldi would deal with that when it happened. "I'm going back up in an hour or so," he told the big Fed. "Can't promise anything, of course, but—"

"Understood," Brognola said. "Whatever you can do. Safely, of course."

Grimaldi had to smile at that. "Safely" meant one thing to your average Joe and something altogether different for those who cast their lot with Stony Man. Jack didn't laugh at danger like a lunatic, but he had long since learned to take the risks in stride, accepting them as part and parcel of his chosen life. When that life ended, he'd be ready for it. Or as ready as a man who cherished every moment of each day could ever be.

"Striker and I have a date in the mountains. I'm not about to stand him up."

"Fair enough. Appreciate it, Jack."

"It's what I'm here for. With any luck, I'll be in touch within a couple hours, one way or another," he said, and ended the call.

With any luck. And if it failed him, Brognola would have to get the news from someone else. The storm would break eventually, but there was no telling how many lives it would claim before the sky cleared.

With that in mind, Grimaldi checked his own GPS locator, made sure it was functioning, and finished off his coffee in a searing gulp. He'd have to file a flight plan, doctored to appease the tower gods, and then he would be on his way.

Into the storm once more.

Holy Trinity Monastery

BROTHER JONATHAN THOUGHT of his family as he plodded toward the monastery's west gate. His parents dead, elder sister confined to a nursing home in Ohio, middle-aged cousins he hadn't seen since he came back from Vietnam. He felt that none of them would recognize him now, dressed in the garb of his profession with a parka overtop, hunting a bunch of homicidal strangers in a blizzard.

Funny. It all reminded him of a bumper sticker he'd seen long ago: Life Is What Happens While You're Making Other Plans.

And wasn't that the gospel truth?

He'd made it halfway to the gate and hadn't seen a soul so far. There was a chance, he thought, that Cooper's frag grenade had taken down the penetration team—or hurt them bad enough to change their minds—but he was still obliged to check it out for sure.

He owed his brothers that, at least.

The cold was getting to him. He could not deny it. Even with the parka and work gloves on, the sub-zero chill was settling in his bones and had already numbed the portion of his face exposed between his hood and his scarf. Although his worst times had been spent in distant jungles, Brother Jonathan had seen frostbite up close and personal, when aged Brother Seamus—no longer with them, bless his soul—had wandered off in a distracted "senior's moment" and gotten lost outside the walls just long enough to lose three toes.

No worries, Jonathan decided. Someone would likely take him out before he had to fret about that.

As if his thoughts could conjure flesh from freezing air, a human shape passed about fifteen feet in front of him, moving from north to south. Lost in the storm? An enemy, in any case.

Almost divorced from conscious thought, Brother Jonathan fired a 3-round burst into the blowing snow, trying to lead the moving figure as they'd taught him all those years ago, in basic training. Felt his heart skip as the target lurched, then fell, giving a squawk that reached Jonathan's covered ears despite the wind.

And then two other guns were firing at him, muzzle flashes dirty orange against the snow's white background, bullets zipping by his head and shoulders. Brother Jonathan dropped instantly, snow cushioning his fall, and rolled to his right as more incoming fire cut lower, searching for him.

For an instant, it was like a waking nightmare of his time in Vietnam—or rather, a negative image of those times: white day versus blackest night, raw cold instead of heat—and he was firing back at more shadows, clutching the unfamiliar weapon, trying to count his rounds and manage his ammo. He wasn't about to let an empty chamber get him killed.

BROTHER THOMAS CLUTCHED the Glock in two cold hands as he advanced toward the abbey's outdoor storm drain, praying that he didn't lose his way when he could barely see an arm's length in front of him. He realized he'd stopped feeling the cold as bitterly since the explosions started, gunfire sounding in their wake.

Get some! The thought came out of nowhere, echoing the invocation for a solid kill he'd heard so often in Iraq that it became his unit's mantra, traded jauntily before a mission, shouted out in battle like a prayer to gods of war.

Their unknown enemies had come to *get some*, and he guessed that they would not retreat until their mission was complete. Cash and fear of a reprisal from their paymasters would keep them pressing forward till the abbey's newest postulant was dead, along with everybody else inside these walls.

Trying to estimate his progress through the snowdrifts was a waste of time. Brother Thomas moved so slowly that counting seconds in his head proved futile.

He thought he had closed the gap to forty yards or so, but even that meant nothing if he'd strayed off course.

This time, at least, he could be sure what he was fighting for: survival and the lives of his adopted brothers in the faith. No profits riding on the line for oilmen or defense contractors sitting safe in offices so posh they put his childhood home to shame. And come to think of it, it *was* a shame: Homewood, a low-rent, crime-ridden housing project that put the *pits* in Pittsburgh. By the time he had been old enough to join the army, swapping one hell for another, Brother Thomas had already seen enough men shot before his eyes to match the body count in any modern action film.

But he'd escaped that, finally. Or so he'd thought.

In front of him, two human shapes appeared. If they were visible to him, he must be visible to them. Dropping to one knee in the snow, so that the drift was piled around his waist, he chose the target on his left and aimed for center mass, planning to turn and catch the shooter on his right if he could manage it.

He pulled the Glock's trigger, and the .40-caliber bucked in his hand, its orange flash instantly imprinted on his retinas as he pivoted a few feet to his right and squeezed off a second round, to catch the shadow on his far right breaking from formation. It was tricky, but he followed through, his third shot on its way before one of the guys he'd tried to ventilate began returning automatic fire.

MACK BOLAN WAITED for any sign of movement around him as he lay in the snow. Since the grenade blast, he'd heard nothing, seen nothing. If his enemies were still alive and moving, they were creeping through the storm, low down, denying him any targets he could recognize.

Snow settled over Bolan as he waited, turning him into a long, low bulge in what was otherwise a level landscape. Were his adversaries lying dead or wounded, yards in front of him, or were they tunneling through the snow, edging closer by the second? He couldn't stay here forever. Even if his enemies didn't find him, lying still in the cold would make him sluggish, leading to slow reaction times, frostbite...or worse.

Whoever was out there in the storm, alive or dead, he had to go and meet them.

Bolan picked a compass point and started crawling toward it. The Steyr, slung around his neck, served as a kind of snowplow, clearing his path with no fear of its closed bolt getting packed with ice. He'd also drawn the Mark I trench knife and was prepared to thrust or slash as needed if he met a solitary enemy head-on.

Bolan estimated that he'd traveled twenty yards or so when his ears picked out a sound beneath the groaning, omnipresent wind. He stopped to listen, and identified the noise as a person crawling through snow, on a collision course for him. Snow crunched as the man approached, and his breathing, though muffled, rasped like sandpaper drawn across smooth wood. Wounded by shrapnel? Winded by the long crawl from the gate? There was no telling until they met and Bolan had a chance to test his adversary's strength.

Waiting, he let the Steyr go and eased his arms overtop of it, so that it wouldn't catch him in the throat when he made his move. He led with the Mark I, ready to strike at the first sight of his opponent. When the creeping form came into view, Bolan was ready.

Like the previous man he'd encountered, this guy was dressed completely in white, with ski goggles cov-

ering his eyes and a mask over his nose and mouth.
But Bolan didn't miss the flinch of surprise as the man
caught sight of him. The intruder clawed at his parka,
pulling out a hidden handgun.

Bolan lunged, stabbing, and felt the trench knife's
seven inches of double-edged steel pierce padded fabric, driving into flesh. The man cried out—whatever
he said sounded like German—and Bolan grabbed his
parka's hood, jamming his face into a suffocating snow
pillow. He held it there, the Mark I still buried in the
man's abdomen, until there were no more tremors of
resistance from his foe.

One more down. And how many left to go?

10

"Is everything secure?" Brother Jerome inquired.

"As best we can prepare it, Father," Brother Francis answered. He was fidgety, out of his element in planning war. The long chef's knife tucked underneath his robe's sash was incongruous, as if he'd decided to impersonate a pirate but had forgotten the other trappings of his costume.

"Doors and windows locked?"

"Yes, Father," said Brother Horatio. His makeshift weapon was a ball-peen hammer, which he held in his right hand.

Brothers Francis and Horatio were covering the abbey's north transept. Teams of two were stationed throughout the Gothic pile, in the south transept, the entrance hall, the dormitory, kitchen, nave and refectory. Monks who had followed Brother Isaac in refusing to shed blood, regardless of the cause or consequences, had been sent to their rooms with orders for unceasing prayer until the crisis was resolved in one way or another.

"Father?" Brother Francis raised a hand, childlike.

"Yes, Brother?"

"If they come...what shall we do against their guns?"

"Your best, Brother," Jerome replied. "Defend the house of God."

"But if we sin on some account—"

"You have my plenary indulgence, Brothers. You have taken on the Lord's work and will not be punished for it, I assure you."

Brother Francis ducked his head and muttered, "Thank you, Father," though he did not sound convinced. Brother Horatio, by contrast, seemed almost at ease, sporting the vestige of a smile. The wisps of hair atop his head, as usual, were snarled and twisted every which way.

"If you need help when the time comes, call for me," Brother Jerome instructed. "I will come to you if I am able. And if not, you have my blessing."

They were spread too thin, he knew. Were too few and far between. Their first line of defense—Matt Cooper, Brothers Thomas and Jonathan—would either stop the enemy outside, or there would be a bloodbath in the abbey, and it was doubtful any of the monks would survive. From the explosions and erratic gunfire he'd heard, it was clear that fifteen monks with a motley arsenal of kitchen knives and garden tools would not last long against their foes.

Continuing on his rounds, Brother Jerome savored the irony of a committed peaceful life ending this way. It was a concept absolutely foreign to him, something he had never once imagined. The Lord might move in mysterious ways, but this was nothing short of surreal.

His next stop was the south transept, guarded by Brothers Lucas and Stephen. They were armed, if he remembered correctly, with a hoe and garden spade. Not much relief against explosives or a hail of bullets, but they would do their best.

And if they died in the attempt?

"*Ego te absolvo a peccatis tuis,*" he intoned, "*sanctus in nomine Christi.*"

It was all Brother Jerome could offer, and despite his deep, abiding faith, it didn't feel like much at all.

BOLAN RETREATED FROM the prowler he had knifed to death, crawling as quietly as he could manage. Someone had likely heard the dying man cry out in German, and wouldn't need a translator to know one of their comrades was in trouble. If they rushed to help him now, Bolan would have targets, but he didn't want to risk being overrun.

He figured twenty feet should do it, far enough away to remain unseen amid the drifting snow, but close enough for him to make out human forms if any gathered to inspect the corpse.

He still had no idea how many men had breached the blown front gates, or whether he had taken out any with his grenade. If he was close on basic numbers, ten to fifteen men required for storming Holy Trinity, he had shaved the odds by 13 to 20 percent. If both his booby traps had taken out one man apiece, call the percentage 20 to 30. Not bad, but still guesswork as long as the blizzard concealed his opponents.

From the distant sounds of gunfire, Bolan knew that

Brothers Thomas and Jonathan had each engaged the enemy. That meant the frag grenades he'd planted earlier had not stopped *everyone* from entering through the west gate or the storm drain, but that was all he could say with certainty. For all he knew, both Thomas and Jonathan might have been cut down within seconds of confronting their opponents. Bolan might be on his own outside the abbey, with nothing but his skill and hardware to protect the monks inside.

And faith? He shrugged it off, trusting in things that he could see and feel.

His Steyr AUG, for instance, cold in Bolan's hands but still prepared to deal out sudden death upon command.

He watched and waited, counting seconds in his head. If any comrades responded to the German's shout, their timing would depend on distance and how well they judged direction in the storm. If they were ultra-cautious, strictly disciplined, they might not come at all. In which case, how long should he wait before he changed tack and started hunting them?

Five minutes, he decided. Anything beyond that was a waste of time that he could better spend checking on Thomas and Jonathan, or scouting other angles of attack for lurking enemies. Four minutes now. He stared into the rippling, ever-shifting wall of white before him. His goggles compromised his peripheral vision, so he turned his head left and right in a regular pattern, eyes constantly tracking. Calling on a sniper's calm, he lay immobile in the snow while more piled up on top of him. He kept his index finger straight beside the Steyr's trigger guard, insurance against accidental discharge that could give away his game.

A subtle movement ahead and to his left captured Bolan's full attention, and he swung the Steyr's muzzle toward it. He dipped his head to use the rifle's telescopic sight, helping to pierce the storm. A vaguely human form lurched toward his fallen comrade, fighting for balance in the wind.

The sniper's index finger curled and came to rest against the Steyr's trigger, slowly taking up the slack.

Twenty thousand feet above the High Sierras

JACK GRIMALDI FELT the Cessna 207 dropping out from under him, and hauled back on the yoke, fighting for altitude before the sudden downdraft could send him plummeting. The little plane responded sluggishly, fighting the vicious wind, but finally responded, slowly climbing, buffeted on every side.

Grimaldi had his sat phone wedged into the copilot's seat, switched on to receive any message that might reach him through the storm. There was nothing so far, but that wasn't evidence that Bolan had been lost in action. Just a void of evidence to reassure Grimaldi that he hadn't been.

Grimaldi was homing on the GPS signals from Bolan's phone and Pocketfinder personal locator, neither one dependent on a live outgoing call. As far as he could tell, riding the roller coaster of the storm, both homers were together, fully functional, and waiting for him just a hair past twenty-seven miles due east. Grimaldi double-checked the coordinates. Bolan's devices, at least, were at Holy Trinity. But whether he was negotiating with the witness, in the midst of battle or shot to ribbons by a team of mercs was anyone's guess from where Grimaldi sat in the cockpit.

So, twenty-seven miles. Right around ten minutes at the Cessna's normal cruising speed, then add some for the headwind he was fighting. Thanks to the storm, he wouldn't be able to see the abbey from above; Grimaldi had only the coordinates and the dual blips from Bolan to guide him there. Landing would be dicey at best, in these conditions. He could only hope that as he descended, visibility would improve, and he'd be able to scout a reasonable spot to touch down. If the snow and wind were this bad at five thousand, even ten thousand feet, he risked smashing into a rock face or being blown out of the sky before he even caught a glimpse of the ground.

But he was almost there and bound to see it through. Grim-faced and grappling with the yoke, Grimaldi held his course.

Holy Trinity Monastery

SOMEONE WAS SCREAMING louder than the wind. Gut-shot, it sounded like, and suffering the pains of hell. A .40-caliber would do that, more particularly hollow-points designed to mushroom on impact and carve a massive wound channel. It could take hours for a man to die that way, unless a bullet or one of its fragments nicked a major artery.

Hours? thought Brother Thomas. I don't have that kind of time.

He'd been successful so far, dodging return bullets from the enemies he'd missed, a spray of automatic rifle fire that would have nailed him if he hadn't rolled aside. Even so, the slugs had passed close enough to rattle Brother Thomas, and he was burrowed down as far as he could get into the snow for cover.

Not that snow would stop a bullet coming his way, but at least he had the vain illusion of concealment. That would shatter when he fired again, but for the moment, Brother Thomas was as invisible as his nearby foes.

"Jesus!" the stricken man cried out. "Help me!"

English, but with an accent: British, possibly Australian. That didn't help Thomas figure out whom he was fighting, but it made no difference. When somebody tried to kill you, you put him down to save yourself, then did your level best to live with it.

Forgive me, Father, for I have sinned.

Or had he? There'd been no time for confession prior to taking up his post, but Brother Thomas figured God might look the other way while he was fighting to defend the abbey and the other Brothers of Saint Faustus. Someone had to do it, and it fell to those with skills they carried from another life, before they'd found the Lord or He'd found them.

The screaming man was about fifteen yards to his left. Brother Thomas thought of crawling over there and ending it, also retrieving whatever the wounded man was carrying—maybe another slick Galil—to even up the odds with his remaining enemy.

But it would be risky. Movement could mark him for a shooter crouching in the snow, waiting to find a target. The man's screams could also be a ruse, an attempt to lure softhearted soldiers—or monks—to their deaths. And even if the man wasn't faking, a companion could be waiting right beside him for some idiot to show himself.

All that, and still Brother Thomas couldn't let it go.

Killing was one thing, but he'd never tortured anyone and didn't feel like starting now. If he could end a poor soul's suffering without committing suicide, and maybe help himself out in the process, Brother Thomas felt the need to try.

He crept forward at an awkward turtle's pace, alert to any intimation of a threat.

"Goddamn it!" the injured man howled ahead of him, cut off by a sob that seemed too real for faking. Brother Thomas thought of ways to end the stranger's suffering without alerting any other shooters in the neighborhood, and all that he could come up with was strangulation.

That is, if his target didn't have a knife.

"Lord, give me strength," he whispered into the storm.

SPIKE O'CONNOR WAS BLEEDING. It wasn't a bad wound, all things considered, but shrapnel had torn through his parka, his jumpsuit and long underwear, piercing flesh in at least six places along his left side from shoulder to thigh. None of the wounds were critical, thanks to his distance from the frag grenade when it went off, but all of them were painful, bleeding through the layers of fabric that prevented him from freezing on the spot.

A frag grenade, for Christ's sake. In a monastery, thrown by someone who knew how to use it.

What kind of crazy freaking monk was that?

A ringer, sure, and well prepared. Not FBI, he was pretty sure, or they'd be bathed in spotlights now, with snipers potting anything that moved. Besides which, there'd been no sign of official vehicles around the abbey when his team made its approach on foot. And since he knew damn well that monasteries didn't tend to feature armed security, what else was left?

O'Connor couldn't waste any more time trying to figure it out. The frag grenade that had peppered him was one of three set off so far, in different quarters of the property. That told him he was facing multiple defenders, or a single man who knew what he was doing. So a soldier, like himself.

And that was bad.

The dying shout from Mueller made it worse.

O'Connor spoke into the mouthpiece of the Bluetooth headset he'd been saving for a dire emergency. "Blake. Jackson. Sordi. Anybody picking up?"

"I'm here, man," Jackson answered in a grainy whisper. "Took a couple hits from that pineapple, but I'm good to go."

"Okay, hang on," O'Connor said. "Blake? Massimo?"

"I'm good," the former Green Beret chimed in.

"I am here," Sordi responded a few moments later, sounding out of breath. "Not well, but here."

Whatever that meant. "Great," O'Connor said. "I picked up half a dozen shards but I'm still mobile." He paused. "We need somebody drawing fire to smoke this mother out."

"Just heard you say you're mobile," Jackson answered. "How 'bout you handle that. We'll cover you."

"I'd rather have somebody else on point," O'Connor said.

"Uh-huh. I figured that."

"Another ten grand out of my end to the volunteer," O'Connor said.

"Make it fifteen, we got a deal," Jackson replied.

"Fifteen it is. Get going."

"You got it, boss."

O'Connor saw Jackson rise out of the snow and stagger forward, step by step. O'Connor didn't focus on the one-time SWAT cop, though, but on the white snowscape around him, where the danger lay.

And he was ready for the muzzle flash, already firing back full-auto as a single shot slapped Jackson off his feet and took him down.

BOLAN EXPECTED A response when he picked off the walker, and he wasn't disappointed. A long Galil burst came at him from the right, punctuated by two rapid twelve-gauge blasts from farther to his left. He ducked and rolled away from most of it, but felt a slug or buckshot pellet strike the steel toe of his boot, a glancing blow that still delivered numbing force.

Bolan returned fire, going for the rifleman first, since he was closer and his weapon's range, coupled with the velocity of the 5.56 mm rounds, made him slightly more dangerous. A 7-round burst rattled away before he swung the AUG around to spot the shotgunner, and heard another *boom* from that direction, coupled with a muzzle flash. Bolan squeezed off another auto burst, at least half his magazine depleted now, then kept rolling before either of his enemies could pin him down.

The shotgun roared twice more, a semiauto model, shredding the snow veils with double or triple O buckshot. The second blast was close, spraying a cloud of powder and ice into Bolan's face. His mask and goggles spared him any injury, and he continued wriggling to his left, letting his adversaries waste their rounds on empty air and snow.

He hammered half a dozen 5.56 mm rounds down range, toward where he'd seen the twelve-gauge muzzle flares, then ducked and rolled again. Was that a cry of pain he heard, or just the blizzard mimicking a human sound of suffering? Whichever, Bolan took a chance and kicked out at the snow behind him, launching himself ten feet forward, frog-style, before he heard the next Galil burst come his way.

No shotgun, though.

Had he been lucky? There was no way to confirm it with the snow screening his vision and another gunman bent on killing him. He'd have to switch the Steyr's magazine out for a fresh one soon, a moment when he'd be more vulnerable to his enemies, defenseless for the seconds he required to pull one mag, replace it, and draw back the non-reciprocating plastic cocking handle on the left side of the AUG's receiver.

Not long, but perhaps enough to finish him.

Away beyond his battlefield, behind the abbey, Bolan heard more gunfire. Two Galils, at least, and something with a larger caliber, maybe the Glock he'd passed to Brother Thomas at their last meeting. He reasoned that there would be no shooting if the monks had both been taken out already, but it felt like wishful thinking. Anybody out there could be firing wild, snow-blind and hoping for a lucky score.

No one took the bait from Bolan's leap, but now he picked out the sound of dragging footsteps, someone approaching cautiously but having a rough time of it. No visual contact yet, but he could track the adversary's progress, more or less, by sound alone. Lying in wait, Bolan let him come. More *pop-pop-popping* from the far side of the abbey told him action there was still unfolding, neither side in charge yet. Bolan still hoped he could stop the predators outside, sparing the monks, but he was far from nailing down his own piece of the property, much less the quadrants held by Brothers Jonathan and Thomas.

One fight at a time. And it was heading toward him now.

11

Halfway to his unseen target, Brother Thomas paused, awaiting further cries to direct him. He had begun to think the man had died without his help, or else tired of the ruse and given up on faking it. Stumped for another plan, Thomas considered creeping back toward the abbey and what passed for shelter there, but he was stopped before he could begin his retreat.

"Help!" cried the stranger, so much closer now. Brother Thomas instantly resumed his forward progress, with a slight correction in his course. The agony behind the man's words seemed genuine enough. Brother Thomas had one job at the moment: find and finish off the stranger he had wounded. After that...

Where was the other gunman? Fear nagged at Thomas, not so much of being ambushed and killed, but of the second gunman slipping past him, entering the monastery to complete his business there. Thirty-three brothers were depending on Cooper, Brother Jonathan and himself to keep the danger out.

What lay in store for Brother Thomas if he let them down?

"Hume, where are you?"

Brother Thomas nearly jumped, the voice was so close. He froze and tried to focus on the snowdrift just in front of him, catching the movement as a body shifted, one leg thrashing. With a concrete target now, he crept alongside it, at arm's length from the wounded man, then reached out with his left hand and clutched the stranger's throat.

The gunman still had strength. He fastened his gloved hands onto Brother Thomas's, trying to pry the strangling fingers from his throat. The man's boot connected with the monk's shin, causing blinding pain where only numbness had existed seconds earlier. Brother Thomas bit his tongue, rose up and swung his right arm back before whipping the Glock down toward the man's face.

The first hit was a glancing blow, but well aimed, grazing the guy's goggles. As Thomas swung again, the stranger let go of Thomas's left hand and flailed to deflect the right, but it was too late. This time the Glock hit dead center, shattering the guy's nose, driving his head deeper into the snow.

Not good enough.

Around the strangling fingers, through the welling blood of flattened nostrils, the wounded man gasped out, "Stop! You're killing me!"

Whatever. Brother Thomas swung the pistol twice more, three times, until all resistance ceased. Even then, he kept his choking grip in place until he felt his adversary shudder and grow still.

During the fight, Thomas had stopped breathing

himself. He gasped for icy air now, shocking his lungs, and rolled back from the body of his enemy. His victim? Had he committed murder? Was that burden on his soul, waiting to be confessed? Though he'd been aware—too aware—of the violence he'd inflicted on the wounded man, it was as if he'd been watching himself from outside his body, operating on instinct and unable to stop himself.

Rushing footsteps startled Brother Thomas from his morbid self-reflection. Sitting up, turning toward the sound, he raised the Glock in both hands, his finger on the trigger. A man suddenly appeared out of the storm, almost on top of him.

Brother Thomas fired three times and saw the runner lurch and stumble before a burst of automatic fire ripped into the monk at point-blank range. Punched backward, Brother Thomas fired once more by reflex, saw scarlet blossom across the rifleman's ski mask, then lost his pistol in the snow.

So this is how it ends? he wondered.

With his last breath, Brother Thomas began the Act of Contrition. "O my God, I am heartily sorry for having offended Thee…"

Eighteen thousand feet over the High Sierras

JACK GRIMALDI HATED FAILURE. More specifically, he hated when elements beyond his control mandated giving up. He'd circled half a dozen times over the spot where Bolan's GPS devices placed him, but the landscape below was totally obscured by blowing snow. The trackers showed no sign of movement, but that wasn't the same as counting Bolan down and out.

Based on the abbey's known coordinates, Grimaldi knew Bolan had reached the target. As to whether he was outside, in the woods or still on the grounds, the pilot couldn't say. He had no visibility, no landing place, no hope in hell of helping, either way. The only thing for Grimaldi to do now was turn around, land at Modesto and report to Stony Man.

Assuming that the storm would let him go.

Flights over the affected area had all been canceled or rerouted by controllers at surrounding airports. Jack had lied about his destination, veered off his projected course, might catch hell for it when he got back. That didn't bother him, but if the tower in Modesto tried to ground him he would have to go over their heads, pull strings, to make damn sure that he retained mobility. That left a footprint, paperwork in triplicate unless somebody used the "C" word—*classified*—and shut the questions down.

He'd think about that later, though. Right now he had to concentrate on staying alive.

He'd flown through hurricanes, typhoons and firefights, but each crisis in the air was different, a brand-new chance to die. Metal fatigue could tear the plane apart. A fuel line might frost over, though they weren't supposed to. Wind shear could remove the Cessna's rudder—or its wings—and send Grimaldi hurtling into the nearest mountaintop without a prayer.

Until that happened, though, he was hanging on for the ride of his life. He kept a close eye on the plane's altimeter, ensuring that a downdraft didn't suck him into a collision course with the looming granite peaks. He had sufficient fuel; his plane was level for the moment, though it was bucking like a ship on the waves.

The 207's creaks and groans troubled Grimaldi, but he had to trust the plane until it let him down.

By which time it would be too late.

Holy Trinity Monastery

SPIKE O'CONNOR YANKED out his rifle's empty magazine and tossed it, no prints from his gloves to trace it if it was ever found and logged as evidence. He inserted another 35-round mag, wishing they'd brought some of the fifties. The longer magazines caused problems firing from a prone position, though, so he'd left them off the shopping list.

No matter. Thirty-five was plenty if he placed them properly and took his opposition out.

Who *was* this guy? O'Connor would have paid five grand to answer that one, but he knew that chance was lost to him. Once killing started, conversation was superfluous, a perilous distraction that would likely get him nothing in return.

Better to kill the bastard and be done with it.

O'Connor's shrapnel wounds were aching now, making him wince at every step he took toward the last spot he'd seen a muzzle flash. The shooter would have moved by now, unless O'Connor had tagged him with return fire, in which case he might be lying dead or dying in the snow.

Let that be it, he thought. For once, just make it easy.

And a small voice answered, Never gonna happen.

Spike hated how the snow crunched underneath his boots, but there was no way to stop it. He hoped that the storm covered the sounds as well as falling snow covered his tracks. He kept his finger on the Galil's

Dark Savior 133

trigger. He had the selector switch on "R"—for "repetition," meaning semiautomatic—to conserve his ammo and accommodate precision fire, assuming such a thing was even possible.

He wished they'd brought grenades, but where would he have tossed them, blinded as he was by sheets of snow? Maybe a flamethrower to blaze a bright path through the storm and give his enemy a taste of hell on earth? Why not artillery while he was at it, letting him sit back a mile or so and bring the abbey crashing down with all hands trapped inside?

O'Connor snapped out of his reverie and focused on the task at hand. He could try to circumvent the gunman who obstructed him, but that would mean leaving an enemy behind him, armed and dangerous. No.

He had to take it one step at a time, eliminate as much risk as he could before the hunt began indoors. Once they were inside the monastery, they might have to go room-to-room. And there were a lot of rooms, according to the floor plan he'd been given. So many places where an enemy could lie in ambush, or where O'Connor's prey could hide.

A sudden blur of movement in front of him and to his right brought O'Connor's weapon into line. He squeezed the trigger twice, a tidy double-tap, but then a muzzle flash erupted, spraying bullets in his direction, and he threw himself facedown into the snow.

BROTHER JONATHAN HAD no trouble with the Galil MAR once he understood that it was modeled on the same Kalashnikovs the Vietcong had tried to kill him with in Nam. Simple, reliable, hard-hitting, it would put his targets down, assuming he could spot them in the storm.

And that, of course, was the problem.

He followed his nose toward the west gate, an old dog running down the scent of Composition B explosive, the familiar mix of TNT and RDX. God knew he'd smelled enough of it when he was younger, in his other life. Granted, the blizzard did its best to spread the smell around, but Brother Jonathan also possessed a fair sense of direction, even if he sometimes passed from one room to another these days and forgot what he was looking for.

Not this time. Today, he was hunting men.

Brother Jonathan was halfway to the gate when he heard voices in the storm. He couldn't pick out words, but there were two guys at least. Getting just a little careless after they'd been blasted at the gate, and likely mad enough to kill without a second thought whoever crossed their path.

No problem there. He knew the feeling.

Once he'd calculated that the voices were approaching him, headed in the direction of the abbey, Brother Jonathan stepped off to one side, three long strides, and knelt down in the snow. He felt the cold abstractly now, his pulse ramping up toward go-time. It was a state he'd been in before, and he welcomed the feeling in a sad and twisted way, but didn't know if he was up to it at this stage in his life. Slower reaction times, a list of chronic aches and pains… He definitely wasn't half the man he used to be.

His weapon, on the other hand, was one hell of an equalizer.

As his targets drew closer, he thought he could distinguish three voices, their conversation demonstrating a lack of discipline that would have had his sergeant spitting nails in Nam. These guys, whoever they were, had come in thinking they would have an easy time of it, knock off some monks who didn't know a rifle's muzzle from its stock, then go and celebrate.

But not just yet.

He had the MAR's selector switch on "R," semiauto. Rather than let the weapon rip and waste his ammunition, Brother Jonathan preferred to time his shots, place them as cleanly as he could, and be ready when the hostiles started shooting back.

And there they were. Three shapes walking abreast, appearing out of the snow like wraiths. He lined up on the nearest man, whispered a prayer that felt like blasphemy, and fired.

BROTHER ISAAC FOUND the abbot primate in the monastery's kitchen, with Brothers Paul and Andrew. They had bubbling pots of oil and water on the range top, with pale steam rising toward the ceiling.

"If they come close enough, Father," Brother Paul was saying, "we thought—"

He stopped at sight of Brother Isaac in the doorway, but did not look away, although the bursar outranked him. Brother Isaac swallowed his anxiety, a hard lump in his throat, and spoke.

"Father, a moment of your time if you can spare it?"

Instead of answering, the abbot told the kitchen's two appointed guardians, "Your plan seems sound and logical. God keep you till we meet again."

The monks both ducked their heads and thanked him for his blessing, as Brother Jerome turned toward the kitchen's exit. Passing Brother Isaac, he said, "I have rounds to make."

The other monk fell into step beside him, fighting an urge to pluck the abbot primate's sleeve. "Can you hear what's happening outside, Father?"

"I'm old," Brother Jerome replied. "Old*er,* that is, but I have all my faculties."

"People are dying, Father."

"I expect so."

"With your blessing!"

Now the abbot primate stopped and turned to face him. "We've already had this argument," he said. "No one has pressed you into service as defender of the abbey. You are free, with those who share your view, to go and exercise the power of prayer. I won't detain you from it."

Brother Isaac refused to be dismissed so easily. "Father," he said, "we still can stop this."

"Can we, Brother? How? By giving up the postulant as Judas sacrificed our Lord? And what would happen to the rest of us in this life, never mind the next? Do you imagine that the people sent to kill us, now that some have dared resist them, will relent out of the goodness of their souls and let us live? How *would* we live with that betrayal, Brother? Would it put your troubled mind and heart at ease?"

Brother Isaac felt angry color rising in his cheeks. "Do you presume to judge me, Father?"

"I judge no one, Brother. I observe and listen." Jerome pointed an index finger toward the ceiling. "He will judge when the time is ripe."

"Regardless of our rank and station, Father?"

"If we're fortunate," the abbot replied. "Now, if you don't mind, I have work to do. Whatever you decide, I hope it brings you peace at last."

With that, he left Brother Isaac alone and moved on toward the dormitory, which was manned by Brothers Carlos and Michael. Standing with his fists clenched, Brother Isaac made a conscious effort to relax, but echoes of the war outside still made him flinch with every gunshot carried on the wind.

BOLAN TRIED TO COUNT the rounds he had expended, but they ran together in the moment, and the Steyr's curved, translucent magazine was frosted over to the point where counting cartridges was problematic. He figured he had two-thirds of the thirty rounds he'd started with before he had to feed the hungry beast again.

So far, he couldn't tell if he'd scored any hits besides the solitary point man who had gone down six or seven minutes earlier. How many soldiers left before he cleared the squad assigned to breach the monastery's gate? Three at least, maybe as many as five.

This battle had turned into a lethal guessing game. Was that a voice, or wind whining inside one of the abbey's gutter spouts? That shadow to his left—was it a man in motion or just rippling drapes of snow? How long before the cold got to his core and started playing hell with his reaction times?

Thirty-something seconds later, at least one question was answered. Apparently coordinated, probably communicating via headsets, three forms rose from nowhere in the blizzard and began advancing toward him at a jogging pace, though they were hampered considerably by the snowdrifts.

Bolan was calculating angles, judging ranges, elbows braced in frozen powder as he peered through the AUG's Swarovski sight, framing each in turn with the telescope's ring reticle. All three figures were more or less the same distance from Bolan, closing slowly in their ragged skirmish line. As far as he could tell, two carried Galil auto rifles, while the third had a longer weapon, probably the shotgun he'd heard earlier. All three were deadly at close range, whether they had a fix on him or not.

He settled on a right-to-left progression since the shooter on his far right was slightly closer. Three strokes of the AUG's progressive trigger sent three rounds off to close the gap between him and his prey. With any luck, he would be fast and accurate enough to drop all three before they could return fire.

With any luck.

He fired and shifted, fired and shifted, fired again. No time to see if any of his targets fell, but one of them at least was firing back, the bullets spitting snow and ice into the Executioner's face.

12

So this was what dying felt like. Despite all his near-death experiences in Nam, Brother Jonathan had not envisioned it in quite this way. He'd always thought it would hurt more, or less, *something* a great deal different.

You never hear the shot that kills you, he thought.

That was total crap, for starters. He'd heard it loud and clear, a shotgun blast, and felt the buckshot ripping into him, his index finger locked around the trigger of his auto rifle, firing as he fell. He'd nailed the man who shot him, saw the figure lurch and drop facedown, then waited for another enemy to loom out of the snow and finish him.

But no one came.

Scared off? He doubted it. Lost in the storm? Or had the rest—however many that might be—proceeded toward the abbey, leaving him and their comrade behind to fight it out?

That thought, the failure of his final earthly task,

gave Brother Jonathan a shot of energy. When he rolled over in the snow, his wound hurt less than he'd expected. It was almost numb now, and he blessed the blizzard for its anesthetic properties. Snow wouldn't stop the bleeding he could feel, all warm and slick inside his robe, but at least he had the strength to rise.

Or so he thought.

The first attempt was damned embarrassing. He made it to his knees, got one foot planted firmly, then the world slid out from under him and he fell on his wounded side. *That* hurt, all right, but Brother Jonathan swallowed the howl of pain. Panting, he tried again, and fell again. At last, he understood that he must crawl to reach the abbey and attempt to help his brothers trapped inside.

With the Galil dangling around his neck, he crept on hands and knees, leaving a dramatic crimson trail behind him that a blind man could have followed if there'd been one in the neighborhood. That made him think of Brother Felix, ninety-something years old if he was a day, stricken with cataracts, who'd memorized the abbey's corridors and never missed a prayer or meal.

The litany ran through Jonathan's mind: God tests no one beyond his strength.

Oh, really?

He had traveled thirty yards from the abbey, give or take. Same distance back, unless he lost his bearings in a moment of delirium, but crawling through the snowdrifts would take much longer. And on top of that, his hands were going numb.

Brother Jonathan recalled a mocking pseudo-prayer from Nam—one of the Psalms, he later realized, pro-

faned by fighting men—and let it play out in his brain
now, meaning no insult to God.

Yea, though I walk through the valley of the shadow
of death, I will fear no evil, for I am the baddest son of
a bitch in the valley.

INCOMING, AND THE twelve-gauge was the worst, raising great bursts of snow while bullets from the two
Galils kicked up their relatively tidy spouts, etching
trails of death in the winter wonderland. Bolan rolled
to his right, breaking the pattern of his last two moves,
and tried to keep track of the muzzle flashes pouring
hostile fire his way.

It nearly worked, until a third blast from the shotgun plastered Bolan's goggles with a spray of icy slush
and briefly blinded him. He wiped them clear with his
sleeve, but that used up a second, maybe two, and gave
his adversaries time to duck, dodge, separate and find
new vantage points.

What now?

He had one last grenade but didn't want to waste it
on a solitary target, especially when the last one hadn't
seemed to slow his opposition down at all. Instead of
chasing hornets with a sledgehammer, he opted for a
more precise approach, if that was possible on this surreal killing ground.

First thing, he had to ditch the Steyr's nearly empty
magazine. The mag release lever was underneath the
rifle's bullpup stock, easy to find and press in darkness
or a blizzard, and he pitched the old magazine away to
his left. Bolan slipped a fresh one from its ammo pouch,
inserted it and pressed another button, just above the
mag release lever, to close the rifle's open bolt.

And he was ready to go. But where had all his targets gone?

Maybe the hunters thought they'd nailed him with their last barrage, and were moving on. Without a clear-cut target, he saw no point in wasting rounds to change their minds. Waiting, on the other hand, was perilous if they had pushed on toward the abbey, focusing on Arthur Watson and the monks inside.

His next move seemed clear: fall back to guard the abbey's entrance as a one-man ambush party.

An enemy who meant to crack the monastery through its front doors had to reach them first, then find a way inside past bolts and bars.

But first, they'd have to get around the Executioner.

BROTHER JONATHAN HEARD gunfire at what he thought was the abbey's back door. It spurred him on to greater speed, though in his present state—wounded and losing blood, exhausted by his creeping progress through the snow—acceleration didn't count for much. His hands and feet were numb now, blunt insensate tools, but frostbite was the last thing on his mind.

He pictured prowlers blasting through the door with automatic weapons, entering the monastery to begin their killing spree. If he survived to reach the entrance—if he even *found* it now without collapsing and bleeding out—would he have strength enough to stand and fight them? Could he even manage lying on the floor and firing at their legs?

He thought about his captured rifle dragging through the snow, then put that out of mind. A weapon patterned on the AK-47 should be able to withstand significant abuse. Israelis would design a gun with desert sand

and grit in mind, not snow and ice, but that was nit-picking. He trusted that the rifle would perform when called upon, as long as he had strength enough to aim and fire it.

First things first. He had to reach the monastery, find the back door—his nose would help him there, tracking the smell of gunpowder—and make his way inside without one of the hunters finishing him off. That was sufficient challenge for the moment, as he labored through the drifts that reached his heaving chest.

Brother Jonathan's mind began to drift, craving the warmth of My Khe beach in Vietnam, Da Nang's recuperation center, and Venice Beach in California, where he'd spent many a drunken night on sand, beneath the stars. Only a tumble saved him from the fantasy, his left hand slipping out from under him to plant his face in cold reality.

With renewed focus, he crawled toward the abbey, starting to believe he'd made a wrong turn somewhere on his blood-strewn journey. It surprised him when his cold hands felt the flagstones of a porch beneath them, partly bared where combat boots had kicked the snow aside. The door gaped open, as he'd feared, and Brother Jonathan reached for its jamb to help him stand erect.

No easy job, that, but he got it done, brushed off his rifle and passed through the door on trembling legs.

ORNELAS WAS DOWN and Gilad Cohen didn't miss him. He had never liked the Mexican; for one thing, Ornelas had aggravated him with constant "jokes" Cohen had rarely understood and never found amusing.

The gash across his cheek, from a grenade fragment, was oozing blood and burning like a hornet's sting imbedded in his flesh. Cohen knew it would be much worse when he removed his ski mask, but for now, the pain kept him alert.

As if he needed that, after he found the unknown gunman gone.

"Where he is?" Denikin inquired.

"Not here," Cohen snapped.

"I see that, smart guy."

"He was hit, we know that much."

The snow was bloody where their faceless enemy had fallen, wounded by Ornelas, and he'd left a scarlet trail as he retreated toward the abbey.

"We should follow him," the Russian said.

"But carefully," Cohen amended.

Wounded men, unless unconscious, were as dangerous as any others on a battlefield. Cohen had no idea who they were dealing with, or why any member of the abbey's brotherhood would have a weapon and be trained to use it, but he did not plan to die here, in a snowfield half a world away from home.

The bloody trail led straight back to the monastery, as far as Cohen could tell. After traveling a few slow yards, hearing more gunfire in the middle distance, he saw the dark bulk of the abbey rear up in front of them. It made him think of movies he had seen in childhood, about madmen and their castles in Romania or Hungary, one of those countries where his ancestors had been betrayed and persecuted in the Holocaust. If he had not been freezing already, staring at it would have chilled him.

Stupid, he thought, and forged ahead, sweeping the white field with his eyes, tracking the blood trail as it veered off slightly to his left.

"There is a door," said Denikin.

"I see it."

Fresh blood led directly to the doorstep. The wounded man had gone inside, presumably locking it behind him. Even if he had not, there was still his automatic weapon, likely waiting on the far side of that door to cut them down.

But they had to get inside. The witness they'd come to eliminate was somewhere in that brooding edifice, along with thirty-odd monks who required silencing. That was supposed to be the easy part, according to O'Connor's briefing, but it obviously wasn't working out.

"You want to try it?" Denikin asked Cohen, nodding toward the door.

"Not after last time," Cohen said.

"What, then?"

"One of the windows, maybe."

There were plenty to choose from, set in stone with leaded muntins, situated about fifteen feet apart. The windows of the upper floors were perfectly aligned with those below. Cohen spotted hinges on the sides, meaning the windows cranked open by hand rather than by lifting a sash. They'd have to break the glass to enter, which meant making noise, alerting anyone nearby to their presence. And they were *small* windows, ready to trap a man carrying bulky, dangling gear.

Disgusted with his options, Cohen turned back to the door. "All right. This way."

"THE SHOOTING'S STOPPED," Brother William observed.

"For now," said Brother Alan, standing in the abbey's entrance hall with the crowbar he had chosen as his weapon.

"Perhaps it's over." Brother William had a claw hammer, gripping it so the claw curved forward like the pick end of an ice ax, ready to pierce skulls.

"I doubt that very much, Brother."

"But you don't know for sure."

"We'll find out soon enough."

The entrance hall was fairly large, its only furnishings a pair of ornate wooden chairs that flanked the massive doors. As far as Brother Alan knew, no one had ever sat in them and none ever would. Why linger in that drafty space, which the boiler barely warmed?

But they had vowed to guard it with their lives, and Brother Alan meant to keep that promise. He imagined striking someone with the crowbar—he who'd never had a fistfight in his life and shied away from arguments—and wondered why he'd volunteered to help defend the abbey.

Simple. It had been his home for thirteen years and he had always felt at ease within its walls.

Until today.

"If someone tries to enter—"

"We prevent them," Brother Alan cut off his companion. "We've been over that."

"But—"

"They have guns. I know. We do our best, with God's help."

"Will He help us? What if He's displeased?"

"You sound like Brother Isaac now."

"He could be right."

"Then go and join him!" Brother Alan snapped.

"I didn't mean—"

"I'm sorry, Brother. This is your choice. If you've changed your mind, go on, but leave the hammer."

"No, I'll stay and—"

Something struck one of the doors, a solid, heavy *thump*. Outside, somebody tried the knob and found it locked. They'd arranged a knock signal with Matt Cooper and Brothers Thomas and Jonathan, so it definitely wasn't them.

"Are you ready?" Brother Alan asked the other monk.

"I believe so. Yes."

Moving to the far side of the left-hand door, which would hide him as it opened, Brother Alan waited, crouching slightly, clutching the cold, curved weapon in his white-knuckled hands.

THEY'D MISSED THE shooter somehow, in the storm. That troubled Spike O'Connor, knowing that the guy was out there, maybe coming up behind them, but they'd wasted too much time already. On the up side, maybe he was wounded, dying in the snow right now, no longer any threat.

Don't count on it, O'Connor thought. "Watch my back," he told Massimo Sordi.

"You're covered."

The door wouldn't open, of course. That was basic, to lock it from inside. He tried both handles, then stepped back. "You have the charges?"

"*Sì.*"

No point in asking. He had watched the Italian lift them from Mueller's corpse.

"Okay. So wire it up."

Sordi stepped past him, kneeling on the snow-swept threshold to attach a C-4 charge, plug in the blasting cap and prime the detonator. He didn't dawdle, his deft fingers working admirably despite the cold.

When it was done, with no sign of any enemies approaching through the blizzard, O'Connor retreated to a safe distance and lay down in the snow, Sordi beside him with his shotgun and the detonator.

"Ready?" Sordi asked.

"Whenever you are."

Half a heartbeat later, the explosion sent a gust of hot air rushing past them, melting snow on contact, plowing a tunnel through the white swirl that surrounded them. O'Connor scrambled to his feet before the echo faded, heard Sordi following close behind as he approached the doors again.

The C-4 charge had done its job, and then some. It appeared as if a pissed-off giant had slammed his fist into the double doors exactly where they joined, splintering wood and shearing off both handles, shattering the lock and smashing through some kind of wooden beam securing both doors from the inside. O'Connor moved through the pungent haze and crossed the threshold, leading with his auto rifle as he stepped into the abbey's entryway.

A hurtling object slashed toward his right temple, but he turned in that direction, ducked and took a glancing blow against his biceps, just below the shoulder joint. If not for swift reactions and the padding in his parka, the attack might well have crippled, even killed him. Falling, he made out a wild-eyed figure with some kind of bludgeon raised to strike again. Was it a crowbar? To his left somewhere, he heard Sordi cursing in Italian, grappling with a second person, one or both of them taking vicious hits. O'Connor focused on his would-be

killer, lifting his Galil and squeezing off a four-round
burst into the madman's chest.

THE HOLLOW BOOM of a C-4 meant one thing to Mack
Bolan: The enemies he'd missed had circumnavigated
him and reached the monastery's tall front doors, had
found them barred, and had removed that obstacle with
sheer brute force.

He missed the detonation's flash, facing the wrong
way into blizzard brightness when it blew, but knew exactly where to go as he turned and made for the broad
front porch. It wouldn't take five seconds for the shooters to pass through the doors once they had blown them,
and he knew Brother Jerome had people waiting at the
threshold.

A burst of auto fire told Bolan that intruders had
discovered the defenders and were killing them. He
took off at a near-sprint, all that the blizzard would
allow for speed.

He was too late, at least for Brothers William and
Alan. He'd met them in passing, as Brother Jerome
reeled off the names of volunteer defenders, and Bolan
had paused to discuss a code for regaining access to the
abbey if he or Brothers Jonathan and Thomas needed
to get back inside.

The monks lay where they'd fallen, one on each side
of the open double doors. A glance told Bolan they had
placed themselves strategically with their tools, a crowbar and a hammer, to attack intruders from their blind
side as they entered. Both had failed, although some
stray blood spatter on the tile floor indicated Brother
Alan might have scored at least a minor blow against
his killer.

Bolan regretted the loss of innocent life, hoped the monks had not suffered too much in their final moments. But he couldn't linger. The only way to honor their sacrifice was to push on, secure the abbey, eliminate the enemy and extract Arthur Watson before any more lives were lost.

The soldier considered his next move. Would his opponents sweep the ground floor first or make their way upstairs? He spotted wet footprints—snow and ice mixed with blood—one set proceeding straight into the abbey's maze of corridors and rooms, the other turning toward a staircase on his left.

Leaving a live opponent on the first floor was a gamble, for himself and every other abbey occupant. But the monks defending the ground floor would have a slight advantage over those above—the kitchen appliances in addition to their makeshift weapons, more places to hide than the exposed, Spartan cells on the upper levels, and several points of escape into the storm if all else failed.

Plus, Arthur Watson was supposed to be upstairs.

Bolan followed the second set of footprints and began to climb the steps.

13

Arthur Watson paced the small room that had been assigned to him on the third floor, southeast corner, wondering how long he had to live. Andrew had left him with instructions not to leave the Spartan cell for any reason whatsoever, then his brother had gone to face the killers who were there only because of Arthur, what he had learned and what he'd tried to do about it.

All in vain, he had realized too late.

He could have simply kept the books for U.S. Global Finance, kept his mouth shut, spent a larger portion of his hefty salary self-medicating any pangs of conscience that disturbed him. When had he become a do-gooder who tried to clean up other people's messes, posing as some champion of truth and justice?

It was all bullshit, he understood, now that he'd dropped the ball and it was rolling over decent people, crushing them to death.

Forgiveness? It was nothing but a fantasy, from where he stood today.

His first impulse was to run, but that was futile. Even if it weren't for the blizzard and the mercenaries who surrounded Holy Trinity—who had already breached the abbey, if he'd interpreted the last loud blast correctly—where would he have gone? The monastery was an aging castle in the wilderness. Regardless of the season, Watson knew he wouldn't last two days alone in the Sierras, wandering in circles until thirst, exhaustion and exposure finished him.

But that would still have been a better end than taking down so many people with him: the three marshals in New Mexico, for starters, then the abbey's thirty-five devoted occupants. Before his lapse in sanity, Watson had never harmed another soul deliberately. Now he would have close to forty on his conscience when he died—including Matthew Cooper, who was one grim bastard in his own right.

All that blood spilled, and for what? Because Andrew didn't have the sense God gave an ant. Because he couldn't simply look the other way.

Most people spent their whole lives looking out for Number One, maybe supporting a family, closing their eyes to other people's suffering. Why couldn't he have been another simple-minded drone and kept his focus on the goal of living to a ripe old age?

Stupid. And it was too late now to double back and make things right—or wrong, depending on your point of view. There were no do-overs in life. You rolled the dice and had to live with it if you crapped out.

One thing he *could* do, though, was join the monks defending the home he'd jeopardized.

But how?

The first thing he needed was a weapon, but he'd

searched his room and come up empty-handed. Never mind that now. He'd pick up something on his way downstairs, even if it was just a pewter candlestick. He'd look for Andrew, hoping they could stand together in the final moments of this sick charade and maybe feel like brothers, one last time.

MASSIMO SORDI CLUTCHED his Benelli M4 shotgun, moving cautiously along a hallway lined with tapestries depicting saints, martyrs and brown-robed monks. His nerves were still on edge from the attack he'd suffered in the entry hall, from a wild man with a hammer teeing off on Sordi's skull.

The lunatic had nearly brained him, too. Only a shout from Spike O'Connor had saved him from the ambush. Falling back, the hammer's claw slicing his left cheek, Sordi had fired a point-blank shotgun blast into the monk's chest and sent him flying like a rag doll in his shredded, bloody robe.

Now Sordi's cheek was throbbing, leaking blood. He had pulled his ski mask off and stuffed it in a pocket of his parka—no point covering his injured face, since they would leave no witnesses alive—but the incessant, bone-deep ache distracted him from his primary task.

Each member of the team had memorized a photograph of Arthur Watson. They would know him anywhere, but that was chiefly useful for identifying his remains. Right now, Sordi's job was to kill anyone and everyone he met inside the monastery. And the ambush at the entryway had taught him not to take for granted that the monks would simply wait to die like helpless sheep.

He had reloaded the Benelli, seven fat rounds in the

magazine, one in the chamber. If he found a group of
monks together, Sordi planned to keep his distance,
take them down with buckshot, then administer a point-
blank coup de grâce to any survivors with his Glock
22. The noise was immaterial; outside the abbey's thick
stone walls, the blizzard raged, and even on a clear day
there were no neighbors in the Sierras.

Sordi supposed the thought of killing monks should
bother him. He had been born and raised a Catholic in
Sicily, but had shed his parents' faith around the time he
was cashiered for executing five civilians in Afghanistan. His squad commander understood that none of
them were trustworthy, but there had been a journalist
embedded with the unit who'd recorded it, and somewhere up the military food chain a captain or a major
had decided an example must be made. Sordi received
no prison time, but he was finished serving as a soldier of Italy.

So what? Today he made more money for one mission than his whole unit had earned in any given year,
and he was free to be himself.

After clearing half a dozen smaller rooms, Sordi
found the monastery's kitchen. It was large enough to
serve a major restaurant, although he thought the stove
and countertops would not have passed a visit from
the health inspector. More pressingly, the room was
occupied.

A fat, balding monk stood before him at the far end
of the room. He had a nervous look, befitting one who
was about to die, eyes flicking restlessly around the
room as if in search of something he had lost. The mes-

sage reached Massimo Sordi's brain too late—goddamn his aching facial wound—and by the time he turned to check his back, another monk was almost upon him.

This one was a wiry, frantic fellow with a long knife in his upraised fist. Sordi tried to parry its descent, but he was too late. The blade, not quite deflected by his shotgun's rising barrel, slid along the weapon's magazine with a grating sound and sliced into his gloved left hand.

Sordi recoiled, cursing, and nearly dropped the weapon. By the time his wounded hand recovered it, the knife wielder had nearly reached him, and he heard the fat monk rushing up behind him, panting as he ran.

HALFWAY UP THE curving stairs, Bolan heard gunfire below. One shotgun blast, seeming to come from one of the larger rooms.

More brothers under attack, he imagined. Bolan thought of turning back, then put it out of mind. He couldn't be everywhere at once, and Arthur Watson was a priority, even if the witness didn't want his help. As far as Bolan knew, only one opponent had made it upstairs so far. Once he'd eliminated him and made sure Watson was secure, Bolan would return to the ground floor and help rid the abbey of its pestilence.

He reached the second floor, where a final footprint led down a hallway, the hunter's trail disappearing on threadbare carpeting. The stairs continued upward. Watson's tiny room was on the third story, but the shooter wouldn't have that information. Bolan strode past the lone footprint in the corridor. He intended to take out the merc before he even set foot on the same floor as Arthur Watson.

SPIKE O'CONNOR KNEW who he was looking for, but *where* to look eluded him. There were dozens of rooms on each floor. It seemed as if the architects had overestimated the appeal of living in the mountains, miles away from anyone or anything of interest, pursuing lives of solemn prayer. If they'd expected droves of applicants, they had miscalculated.

No great shocker there.

He'd cleared five rooms so far, was starting on the sixth, and hadn't seen another living soul since the attack downstairs. He guessed most of the monks were hiding out somewhere, maybe divided between chapels or below ground, perhaps in catacombs, with a select few left topside, standing guard duty. He was required to search the whole place, nonetheless, to verify that Arthur Watson wasn't hiding in a closet, laughing up his sleeve.

So far, he had nothing to show for it.

The next door on his left was marked Scriptorium. O'Connor flung it open, ensuring that it struck the wall to deal with anyone who might be hiding back there, but there was no ambush. Instead, he found five solemn monks regarding him from seats around a table, hands joined.

A slender monk rose, releasing the hands of those on either side of him. In a tremulous voice, he said, "I am Brother Isaac. We are praying to be left in peace."

Good luck with that, O'Connor thought. "You want peace, give us Arthur Watson."

"You intend to murder him?"

"What's it to you? You've only known him for a couple days."

"He has requested to become a part of our community."

"I bet he has. You smart enough to know when someone's using you for cover?"

"God forgives—"

"I don't." O'Connor cut him off, raising his auto rifle's muzzle toward the table as he emphasized the point. "My men and I are here for one thing. Do yourselves a favor. Give it up instead of fighting us."

"Those of us here voted against the use of violence," said Brother Isaac.

"Good for you. I still need Arthur Watson, front and center. Where's he hiding?"

"Sir, we have a duty to the Lord. Our vows demand—"

"So that's your final word, then?"

The monk swallowed down whatever else he meant to say, scanned the faces at the table and answered, "It is."

"Well adios, then," Spike replied, and sprayed the table with his MAR, pitching the four monks from their chairs, toppling their spokesman over backward, fogging the tableau with scarlet mist.

No monks had been assigned to guard the west door from the inside, since Brother Jonathan had been stationed on the outer threshold and the rest were spread too thin already. That had been a relief—no corpses sprawled in lakes of blood to greet him as he'd hobbled in, barely able to stand. Jonathan was deep inside the monastery's maze of corridors now, his rifle getting heavier with each step, and there were no targets in sight.

How long did he have? From the way he felt—shaky, chilled to the core, still losing blood—a quarter of an hour would be generous. Five minutes felt more like it, but he had to wring the final ounce of strength from his failing muscles before giving up the ghost.

To keep himself upright and moving, Brother Jonathan relied on the wall to his left, slumping against it while his wooden legs propelled him forward, parka whispering against the plaster to announce his progress if his enemies were listening. He'd be an easy mark, but he was out of options now. He could either keep on going with a wounded old man's shuffle, or sit down and die.

Not yet.

He had been wounded twice before—another time, another war—and once possessed the Purple Hearts to prove it, till he'd pawned them in L.A. to fund his last great binge. They had been flesh wounds both times, nothing that could match his present injury. This one was killing him, he understood instinctively. It was beyond the skills of Brother Thaddeus, the abbey's medic, and there'd be no trip to town for treatment that could save his life.

Not every man was privileged to recognize the place and hour of his death, and fewer still were granted opportunity to make it count for something, helping others in their final moments. If his sacrifice allowed some of his brothers to survive, it would be worth it. Otherwise…

He reached a dead end, with passages branching off to his left and right. He had a choice to make.

Brother Jonathan checked both ways, saw no one and turned left, because it let him stay in contact with the wall supporting him. His mouth and throat were parched, and now that he was warmer, he'd begun to feel as if he had a fever. One more inconvenience to cloud his senses, slow him down and make him vulnerable to mistakes.

"Lord, give me strength," he whispered.

BROTHER ANDREW STOOD over the man he'd slain with help from Brother Paul. He'd buried the chef's knife in the dead man's chest while they were grappling in the doorway, before Brother Paul had clubbed the gunman with a frying pan and brought him down. They'd stood together, watched him breathe his last breath, and all Brother Andrew felt was sweet relief.

"We need to move him," Brother Paul said. "Get him out of sight. There may be others coming soon."

It made good sense, and Brother Andrew took the corpse's feet, while pudgy Brother Paul, significantly stronger than he looked, grabbed two handfuls of the gunman's parka and hoisted the lolling head and shoulders.

"Walk-in freezer?" Brother Paul suggested.

"Good enough for now."

The distance was only twenty feet or so, with Brother Paul inching backward, glancing frequently over his shoulder to avoid colliding with the stove or long island in the middle of the kitchen. Arriving at the freezer, he was forced to set his burden down, open the door, then lift the dead man once again and waddle inside.

The freezer shelves were full, well stocked for winter, so they left the gunman stretched out on the floor. Brother Andrew retrieved his knife, placing one foot atop the corpse's chest and tugging with all his might to free the blade. That done, he found the dead man's pistol, with spare magazines, and handed them to Brother Paul.

"What should I do with these?"

"Defend yourself. It's better than a skillet."

The other monk nodded.

When they had shut the freezer's heavy door, Brother Andrew tossed his bloody knife into a nearby sink and went to fetch the prowler's shotgun. Long ago, he'd done some skeet shooting, and while he'd never been an expert at it, he remembered one good thing about a shotgun: when it fired, the pellets spread, meaning you didn't have to be the world's best marksman to achieve a hit.

A thought occurred to him. "I'll be right back," he told Brother Paul.

"Where are you going?" his companion inquired, sounding alarmed.

"The freezer. He should have more ammunition for the twelve-gauge somewhere underneath his coat."

BOLAN HAD CLEARED most of the north wing on the abbey's second floor when automatic gunfire from the south wing drew him from another empty room into the north-south corridor. No one was visible, and it was difficult to judge his distance from the sound's source, with so many intervening walls and high ceilings battering the echoes back and forth.

The hallway was about three hundred feet long, which narrowed down the possibilities. Toss in an echo factor, and the shots might have been fired somewhere within the east or west wings of the second floor, but

Bolan doubted it. There'd been a certain resonance that persuaded him his goal lay straight ahead.

Moving along the hallway past the rooms he'd cleared, he watched for any movement up ahead. No one emerged from any doorway, but Bolan knew that was no guarantee of safety. He'd found that some rooms had connecting doors to others. At the rear of one small chapel he had found a passageway concealed behind the altar, and while Bolan had not followed it, he saw that it would lead him toward the staircase that had brought him to the second floor.

His first impression had been right: for all its evident simplicity, the monastery was a maze.

Bolan cleared the crossroads where the hallways met, no opposition lurking on either side, and made his way into the south wing. There, instead of clearing rooms as he proceeded, he followed his nose, an olfactory trail leading him to the source of gun smoke. A door labeled Scriptorium stood open to his left, and Bolan edged inside to meet a scene of carnage.

Five monks sprawled around a table where they had been seated when they died. Bolan knew only one of them by name: Brother Isaac, who had led the opposition to an armed defense of Holy Trinity. The brother's pacifism had not saved him in the end, but Bolan couldn't say that fighting would have served him any better in the face of modern military weapons.

What he could say, with a fair degree of certainty, was that the man who'd killed those unarmed monks had not left the scriptorium through access to the north-south corridor. Bolan's response had been too quick for that. Which meant...

He found the other door behind a set of shelves

supporting reams of stationery. It opened on another, smaller hallway running parallel to the main corridor. A glance inside showed no retreating forms to the north or south.

A gamble, then. Bolan turned left, hoping he was not mistaken as he set off in pursuit.

14

Colin Hume was fucking angry and he didn't care who knew it. There'd been no communication from their so-called leader, Spike O'Connor, since a cryptic "We're in" about ten minutes earlier, which did Hume and his Aussie sidekick, Hitchener, no damned good at all. At least the cold and wind stung less with his blood boiling.

Hume had been taught to improvise and deal with obstacles, of course, when he was training for the Special Air Service at Hereford, on the River Wye. And he had proved himself in both Afghanistan's howling wasteland and Libya, most recently. He'd been judged "overzealous" for his grilling of Libyan soldiers in the field, so here he was, freezing his bollocks off to kill a fugitive accountant and a bunch of monks, covered in gore from the team member who'd blown up in his face.

Was life a crazy pile of shit, or what?

"We've got a door here," Hitchener said, and gestured with his MAR to emphasize the point.

Hume saw it now, through the swirling snow, just

where it should be, based on floor plans of the abbey they had studied on the flight to California. It opened onto the refectory, which Sordi had told him was the monks' mess hall. There would be no more meals served today, and Hume was hoping they would find the large room empty, allowing them to access the abbey's labyrinth of hiding places, But he wasn't taking anything for granted.

And, of course, the door was locked.

"Dead bolt?" Hitchener asked. There was no keyhole on their side to suggest otherwise.

"Or barred, a place like this," Hume said. "Who knows?"

"Plan B, then, eh?"

"Plan B."

They both stepped back and leveled their Galils, set full-auto, ripping 9-round bursts into the sturdy, unmarked door. That done, Hume tried again and felt the door move against the faint resistance of what he supposed to be a shattered wooden bar.

"Do we trust this?" the Aussie asked.

Hume thought about it. "I can't believe they have a stockpile of grenades."

"Your go, then."

The Brit held his breath and kicked, cleared the doorway, spilling pale electric light into the storm. In front of them, two monks stood waiting on the far side of a sturdy trestle table they'd tipped over to form a kind of barricade. One held a garden hoe as if he were a pikeman from medieval times. The other clutched a hatchet to his chest.

Pathetic. Neither one of them was Arthur Watson.

Hume saw no good reason to negotiate, but felt he

had to ask, regardless. "Where's the rat we've come looking for?"

"I don't know who you mean," the hatchet man replied.

"You're bloody useless then," Hume said, and shot him in the chest.

Hitchener took down the other monk without a second thought, and they moved on.

THE LEFT TURN from the scriptorium had been instinctual. Bolan calculated that the gunman he was tracking had already neared the far end of the abbey's southern hallway on the second floor. It made sense for him to retreat to the stairs, either to check the floor above or to descend and help his comrades scour the ground floor and labyrinthine cellars. If he found another corridor to follow on the second floor, maybe he'd leave a door ajar to mark his path.

Maybe.

Meanwhile, more shots reached Bolan's sharp ears from a distance, somewhere below him. Rifles, or a single weapon firing twice in semiauto mode, which offered two potential explanations: either monks were dying, or his lookout, Brother Jonathan, had made it back inside the monastery and was hunting down intruders.

Bolan knew which scenario he liked the best, and which was the more likely to be true.

And there was nothing he could do about it now.

Hard choices were a daily part of Bolan's life, had been since he came home from military service to the ruins of his family, and chose a path of vengeance that expanded into a lifelong crusade. Goals were established and prioritized. A soldier either worked his mission or he risked losing it all, losing himself.

None of the doors lining the access corridor were labeled, but he found two standing open. Bolan checked the one to his left and found himself in a storeroom lined with shelves loaded with rolls of paper towels and toilet tissue, cleaning products, household tools and bright spools of extension cord. He was the only occupant.

Returning to the hallway, Bolan went back to the other open door and nudged it wider with the muzzle of his Steyr AUG. A cautious glance, allowing for the blind spot to his left, showed a flight of service stairs he hadn't seen before.

The question now was whether to go up or down.

In Bolan's mind, the same logic applied as when he'd trailed his enemies into the monastery. They'd split up to search for Arthur Watson, killing witnesses as they encountered them along the way. The one who'd gone upstairs would keep ascending, Bolan thought. Without clearing the third floor, his ascent would be a waste of time.

So, up it was.

Bolan moved toward the stairs, checked them as far as he could see in both directions, then began to climb.

Three minutes, give or take, had passed since he'd heard any shots downstairs. With each step he took, ascending to the abbey's topmost floor, he dreaded an explosive fusillade that would announce another massacre of innocents. His focus still remained on Arthur Watson, but he had to wonder if the CPA was worth the blood already shed on his account, or that which would be spilled before the Executioner was done.

ARTHUR WATSON HAD retrieved a fireplace poker from an empty common room along the way between his sleeping chamber and the main stairs leading to the second floor. It was a wrought-iron piece, a simple pointed rod with one barb near its tip for snagging logs. If used correctly, it could be a spear or bludgeon.

Either way, it wouldn't do much good against machine guns like the one he'd heard firing downstairs.

Watson presumed he was as good as dead, and once he had decided that, a measure of his fear melted away. Not *all* of it—he wasn't crazy—but at least he'd dredged up nerve enough to fight instead of hiding in a closet, waiting for the end he'd brought upon himself and those who tried to shelter him.

He stepped onto the landing and saw a shadow coming up the flight below him on the U-shaped staircase, stretching up the wall. The climbing figure, still invisible from where he stood, moved with assurance, and he saw the outline of a shadow weapon jutting over one broad shoulder.

Watson instantly retreated to the first door on his right and slipped inside, one more of the abbey's cell-like bedrooms that outnumbered its inhabitants. He left the door open an inch or so, to better hear his enemy approaching, and stood waiting with the poker clutched in both hands and cocked above his shoulder like a baseball bat, ready to swing with every ounce of fevered strength he had.

"I HEAR SOMEONE COMING," Brother Lucas said.

"Father again?" asked Brother Stephen.

The two of them were concealed in the shadows of monastery's south transept. Two more monks, Horatio and Francis, were stationed a hundred feet from them, in the north transept, while Brothers Leonard and George hid behind the pulpit in the nave.

Though the enemies they faced were not looters per se, and there was nothing much worth stealing in the nave because the Brothers of Saint Faustus had taken vows of poverty, there was principle involved.

The congregation gathered here five times daily for their rituals of prayer and song. If the intruders took the nave, they would effectively command the monastery.

"No," Brother Lucas whispered. "There's two of them. They're talking."

"Couldn't that be our brothers?" Stephen asked.

"No," said Lucas. "These sound foreign."

He held a kitchen mallet with a wooden handle and a spike-faced head of steel, for tenderizing cheap cuts of meat. Brother Stephen had an eight-inch carving knife in one hand and a smaller steak knife in the other, neither of them ranking as impressive weapons against firearms.

"I believe they're coming this way," Brother Stephen whispered.

"Yes."

"Should we deploy?"

Brother Lucas peered across the shadowed nave and thought he saw the others slipping from their hiding places, moving in among the rows of simple wooden pews. It was the plan the six of them had hatched together, setting up an ambush that would likely end with all of them stone dead.

But they would do their best.

"We should," he answered, and set out, crouching as he proceeded to the row he'd chosen in advance.

He dropped to his hands and knees when he got there, crawling toward the central aisle and being careful not to let his mallet scrape the concrete floor.

He did not check on Brother Stephen, knew the frightened monk would do his duty, drawing on God's strength if he was able. They were human sacrifices, Brother Lucas supposed, a concept not unknown to Christianity by any means. But if he was correct about the number of their enemies, if it was four-on-two, there was at least an outside chance they might get lucky.

Lucky? Killing in the house of God?

In its defense, he corrected himself, and he let it go. The fight awaiting him demanded every ounce of concentration he had.

Their enemies were in the nave now, boots clunking along the aisle, the gunmen doubtless checking every row of pews as they passed. The mallet seemed to take on weight as Brother Lucas squeezed its handle, knuckles blanched and aching, bracing for the first swing that would likely seal his fate.

He had to leap before the armed intruders saw him, or he'd never have a chance. Legs coiled beneath him, tingling while he tried to judge the targets' distance from his hiding place, he said a silent prayer and wished there had been time for a confession of his sins.

A shadow fell across his pew then, and he sprang erect, howling in righteous rage, his mallet whipping toward a startled face.

HALFWAY UP THE second flight of U-shaped stairs, Spike O'Connor froze and listened. He'd heard something—muffled shouting, he thought—but now he couldn't say whether the sound had issued from above him or below.

Likely some other members of his crew were busy killing monks, but it still put his nerves on edge.

As if they weren't already, from the fight outside, the ambush in the entryway and now his creeping hunt for Arthur Watson.

He'd been foolish, thinking this would be an easy mission, even with the weather as an obstacle. O'Connor had imagined entering the monastery, rounding up the brothers and their wanted guest, annihilating them and heading back the way he'd come, leaving their dirty secret to the blizzard, and picking up a nice lead while the roads were clogged with snow.

Reality was something else entirely.

He had lost three men for sure—a quarter of his team—and likely more, based on the unexplained explosions that had rocked the abbey's western and northern entry points. Packing them out would be impossible, which meant he'd have to sanitize the corpses before leaving them behind: destroy their faces, teeth and fingerprints, tattoos and major scars beyond the capability of any forensics lab in the world to reconstruct. That would be butcher's work, but he could share it with the members of his team who still survived.

And what if I'm alone? he thought.

The answer was immediate: Screw it. Use C-4 charges on the bits that matter. Burn the rest.

Not easy, but effective. He could manage it, would never be mistaken for a squeamish Sally, and he knew enough to drive the snowcat back to town, as well. By the time police entered the abbey, he would be on a warm beach somewhere. The Caribbean, maybe Belize.

O'Connor resumed his ascent to the third floor, reached it moments later and paused there, inspecting the choices before him. The corridor branched from the landing, one arm leading north, while the other kept on going east, then hooked a right turn and vanished. He decided on the closer hallway first and headed in that direction, counting closed and silent doors.

He'd have to check them all, and make damn sure no one was sneaking out behind his back.

"Get on with it," he muttered to himself, and reached for the first doorknob on his left.

BOLAN HEARD THE distant din of battle from the ground floor, sounding primitive until a pair of automatic rifles stuttered into it. From there, some of the fighting cries turned into wails of pain, nothing he hadn't heard a thousand times before.

He'd learned to live with that, but never quite got used to it.

It would have helped if he could shout for Arthur Watson through the abbey's corridors, but that was obviously out of bounds. By now, he guessed, the hunters who'd survived to reach the monastery proper were dispersing throughout Holy Trinity, stalking their man, eliminating any others whom they met along the way. Maybe one of the monks would babble to the killers in extremis, tell them where the fugitive was hidden. In that case, a small mob could be headed Bolan's way and he would have to deal with it.

Below him, louder now and seeming closer, battle sounds echoed beneath a vaulted ceiling. Possibly the lobby, with the action spilling out of where? The nave was nearest, but he found it hard to picture any fighting to the death in the hallowed space.

The chainsaw sound of a Galil on auto fire turned

shouts to screams down there, but someone still kept fighting back. Bolan wouldn't have called it triumph of the spirit, but at least some of the monks were standing their ground.

And dying, by the sound of it.

Closing his mind to the carnage on the ground floor, Bolan climbed the last few stairs to reach the third-floor landing and resume his search.

BROTHER JEROME WEPT for his soul and for the others in his charge. The private chapel where he knelt before a stature of the Savior crucified was barely closet-sized, reserved for use of the abbot primate alone, and today it smelled of desperation. In his mind, Brother Jerome believed that he had failed his brothers, failed his church and failed himself.

The tortured face of Christ overhead seemed to agree.

The abbot's prayer was rambling and disjointed, nearly incoherent even to his own ears, but he trusted in the Lord to understand and recognize his anguish.

Everything Brother Jerome had worked for and achieved since taking on the leadership at Holy Trinity was crashing down around him. He could not have said how many brothers were already slain, for he had not gone out among them since his first walk-through, encouraging the troops, sparring one final time with Brother Isaac, all in vain. Jerome might be lucky if the church declined to excommunicate him posthumously for his failure at the abbey, all its good works drowned in blood.

He could have turned the fugitive away—should have, perhaps—but he'd allowed his sympathy for

Brother Andrew, plus the church's long tradition of providing sanctuary to the lost and hopeless, to prevail over his common sense. The cost of that decision now was death on a massive scale.

Begging forgiveness from the Savior sounded hollow and futile in the face of the catastrophe ongoing under God's own roof. Brother Jerome believed he should do *something,* but the truth was that he feared to take the final step and sacrifice himself.

But in the last analysis, what difference did it make? He could die fighting with the brothers who remained, or he could wait here on his knees for one of the invaders to discover him and kill him at the feet of Jesus, weeping like a helpless child.

"Thy will be done," he said at last, and struggled to his feet, knees aching from the cold stone floor.

The weapon he'd selected, a barbaric-looking cleaver from the kitchen, occupied the tiny chapel's single pew. He picked it up and weighed it in his hand, perhaps three pounds of steel and plastic, with a bulky nine-inch blade, and drew his thumb along the cutting edge, leaving a smear of blood.

So be it.

He would go forth, find whichever brothers still survived, and lend his hand to their last struggle with the enemy. If death awaited him, and hell beyond it, he would willingly accept that as his due.

He left the chapel door open behind him, just in case some other lost soul happened past and felt a need to pray.

15

Bolan paused to check his surroundings. The abbey's top floor was dimly lit, ceiling fixtures every forty feet burning low-wattage bulbs. Part of the budget crunch at Holy Trinity, Bolan thought, or maybe just a mood-setter for thoughtful contemplation on the great questions of life and afterlife.

He didn't know how many of the third floor's rooms were occupied on a normal day, let alone this day when nothing was even remotely normal. Brother Isaac had suggested that the monks on his side, those opposing armed resistance to the hunting party, stay in their cells and pray, while he and four or five like-minded brothers gathered for communal prayer to touch the mercenaries' hearts. That obviously hadn't worked, but as for the dispersal of the pacifists, Bolan had no idea where to expect them or if he would find them alive.

Dim halls stretched away from him in two directions when he stepped out of the stairwell, doors along both sides. He would have to clear each one in turn, unless he chose to call out Arthur Watson's name aloud, a plan that struck him as sheer lunacy.

He started to his left and found two empty rooms—one with a cot and basic furniture, the other bare from wall to wall—before he met another living soul. The third room's occupant, a youngish monk he didn't recognize, was kneeling when he entered, but sprang up and dodged into a corner when the white-clad figure filled his doorway.

"Please, sir, don't—"

Bolan cut short the useless groveling. "Relax. I'm on your side," he said, and closed the door behind him as he left the chamber, which was rank with fear.

He cleared another three rooms, empty, then surprised another solitary monk. This one was older, with a mop of graying hair, and Bolan vaguely recognized him from the gathering downstairs, before all hell had broken loose. The robed brother was sitting on his cot, hands clasped, and forced a smile of sorts at the sight of Bolan on his threshold.

"It's not going well downstairs," he said.

"I can't say, but they could have used more hands," Bolan replied.

"Not mine. It seems a coward is no use to anyone, not even God."

Bolan nodded grimly, turning away.

"You're looking for the postulant?"

"That's right."

"He's in the other wing, unless he's run away by now. It's tempting, but where would I go?"

Instead of answering, Bolan stepped out and closed the door, heading toward the other hallway.

THE AMBUSH IN the nave went well enough, for ten or fifteen seconds, then it turned into a melee so disorganized that Brother Leonard had no clear idea of what was happening: gunfire and blood, slashing and falling, supplications to the Lord and filthy curses, cries of pain and fear.

He'd crept down from the dais with Brother George as they'd planned, joining the others from the north and south transepts and melting into the rows of empty pews. It seemed to Brother Leonard that the rustling of his woolen robe was loud enough to wake the dead in the abbey's catacombs, and in that moment he was moved to wonder who would bury him.

Expecting failure was a flaw of his, he realized. But honestly, what hope did any of them have against trained men with guns?

Exodus 14 said, "The Lord will fight for you; you need only to be still," but where exactly was He, right now? Maybe hovering around the ceiling beams somewhere, but if He planned on striking down their enemies, the time was now.

Brother Leonard wished he'd found a better weapon than the garden spade he carried, but it had a certain versatility. The round tip was sharp enough to stab with, the two thin edges of its blade could be used for hacking, and the D-handle was designed for thrusting. If he managed to achieve surprise and struck decisively the first time out, there was a fair chance he could drop one of the armed intruders.

And then what?

Seize his firearm? Try to figure out its mechanism before someone else stepped up to kill him?

He didn't have to face that decision, as it turned out.

The brothers from the transepts had been closer to the abbey's enemies as they advanced into the nave, leaping from where they had concealed themselves and rushing to attack. Brother Leonard had missed the moment, uncoordinated as it was, while whispering a prayer for strength. He rose in time to see one of the prowlers fire a bright, ear-splitting burst into Brother Horatio at point-blank range, and then the battle joined, degenerating swiftly into chaos.

Brother Leonard sped forward, robe flapping around his legs, his spade held out like a lance.

He'd seen the second gunman fire at Brother Lucas, grazing one of his arms, and then retreat as he weighed the odds. The shooter had called out to his comrade, who was busy handling his own fight, farther down the aisle. When Brother Leonard reached him, jabbing with his spade, the tip bounced off his target's parka, and he watched the smoking muzzle of the stranger's automatic weapon swing toward his face.

BROTHER JONATHAN WAS worn-out by the time he encountered the enemy. It was pure, dumb luck that he came up behind, rather than facing them, two men pausing to discuss the abbey's layout as they went hunting. Brother Jonathan moved up behind them, bracing himself against the wall to stay more or less on his feet.

Both men heard him coming, turned to face the sound, and Brother Jonathan squeezed off a hasty burst without stopping to aim, not altogether certain he could lift the rifle to his shoulder if he'd wanted to. He missed, of course, and wasted half a dozen bullets in the process, and it made the intruders split up, ducking off to either side of the corridor and dropping into crouches they'd rehearsed in drills and probably in combat.

Cursing like the soldier he'd once been, and instantly regretting the transgression, Brother Jonathan surrendered to the pull of gravity and landed on his backside, buying precious microseconds with the sole defensive move he could manage. Both his opponents fired together, bullets cutting through the air where he had stood a heartbeat earlier, and he returned fire toward the closer foe, using every bit of strength he still possessed to level the Galil.

A splash of blood rewarded him, his target lurching backward, his left cheek exploding. The guy hit the ground, heels drumming on the concrete floor. Brother Jonathan was already swinging his rifle toward his second enemy, still firing out of fear he would lose the weapon if he eased up on his trigger. Wasting rounds, but there was nothing he could do about it now.

The second shooter saw it coming, rolled, and gutted Brother Jonathan with half a dozen slugs that bounced him off the wall and left him sprawled out on his side, the rifle beyond his reach.

Jonathan closed his eyes and hoped that some of what he had been taught, at least, was true.

ARTHUR WATSON WAS expecting death at any moment, but he got a brief reprieve when his would-be assassin began his search of rooms along the third floor corridor with one across the hall from where the fugitive accountant had concealed himself. He waited, trembling, with the fireplace poker cocked and ready to swing. He heard the other door open, then close, with nothing but silence to follow.

More waiting. What was taking the gunman so long?
The rooms up here were small, identical in their sparse
furnishings, with open clothes cupboards in place of
closets. There was nowhere for a man to hide in any of
them except underneath a cot, where he would be read-
ily visible from the doorway.

Finally, after what seemed like an eternity, Arthur
heard the door open and close again quietly, as if the
searcher meant to take his time and cut out all unnec-
essary noise. The problem now was where he would
go next: across the hall to Arthur's hiding place, or on
along the corridor, clearing one side before he doubled
back.

For God's sake, Watson thought, just get it over with.

His almost-prayer was answered. Footsteps approached his door. He took a step back, hunching forward with his poker raised, his buttocks almost pressed
against the wall behind him. Arthur took a deep breath
and held it, ready to put everything he had behind the
swing.

The doorknob turned, nothing to stop it, since the
sleeping rooms, while offering a modicum of privacy,
could not be locked from either side. The door began to
open slowly, inch by creeping inch. Arthur had turned
the lamp off, and there was no window. Dim light was
spilling into the room now, a wedge expanding as the
door moved farther back.

A shadow fell across the threshold, the same one
he had seen mounting the staircase earlier. His lungs
were close to bursting from the breath he held, and dark
motes danced before his eyes. His hands had suddenly
gone numb, making him fear he'd drop the poker before he had a chance to strike his enemy. Or would his

trembling legs give out first, dropping him to the unforgiving floor?

A rifle came into the room before its owner, muzzle sweeping back and forth. Panic and oxygen starvation seized control of Arthur Watson then, making him lash out with the poker, striking steel instead of flesh, jarring the weapon from his adversary's hands.

ALEKSEI DENIKIN SAW Gilad Cohen fall, brained by a shovel-wielding monk, and he shot the robed madman from where he stood, five paces away. That helped no one, least of all the downed Israeli, who already had another monk on top of him, stabbing him in the throat with what appeared to be a screwdriver or chisel.

Where had they all come from, slashing with their makeshift weapons like a pack of human jackals?

There'd been no one visible inside the nave when he and Cohen entered, checking out each row of pews in turn. Dim lighting helped the home team, naturally, since they knew their way around the place, but Denikin had sharp eyes and had seen nobody creeping out to ambush them as he'd advanced along the sanctuary's center aisle.

Now they were everywhere. Two down that he was sure of, one hacking at Cohen's corpse, three more rushing at Denikin with weapons raised to strike. He fired a burst in their direction, jerked the trigger when he should have squeezed it, knowing that his rounds were high and wasted even as they left his rifle's muzzle. All the monks did was duck and keep on coming.

Denikin needed a place to stand and fight, but running backward wasn't half as easy as it seemed in theory, with lunatics pursuing him. He veered off course, collided with a pew that bruised his backside, tripped him, sent him toppling onto the cold concrete. He rolled and bounced back to his feet, barely in time to save himself, a sharp blade nicking his brow before he knocked it away and sent it flying into the shadows.

Then the Russian turned and bolted. It was all he could think to do in the circumstances. He wasn't trying to escape, but to put space between himself and his attackers, so he could turn and rake them with a whole damned magazine, then draw his Glock and finish it up close, when those he hadn't killed were lying helpless at his feet.

He heard the pack behind him as he ran. It was damned savvy of those monks to stage an ambush as they had, taking their losses but eliminating Cohen, nearly dropping Denikin in turn. Warm blood was flowing into his right eye, half blinding him when he could least afford it, but the rough plan he had in mind was simple. It required no expert marksmanship, just nerve and grim determination to survive.

Denikin almost made it.

He was almost at the nave's threshold when suddenly a shadow loomed in front of him, a man his own size, maybe bulkier, but hooded, so Denikin could not make out his face. He saw the upraised cleaver, though, descending toward his skull, with no time left to even raise his hands.

COLIN HUME WAS on his own and hating it, wishing he'd stuck with Spike O'Connor for the search instead of splitting up. It had been Spike's idea, of course, and it had sounded fine at first. But now that they were separated, things were going wrong. He heard fighting, not so far away, although he had no view of the combatants and couldn't put a name to any of the voices crying out in pain or rage.

Somehow, the monastery had become a battleground, when it was meant to be a slaughter pen.

Hume didn't mind the rough stuff, but if given a choice, he liked his targets docile and unarmed, the proverbial sitting ducks. It made life easier, and that way he got paid for doing next to nothing.

This was different, beginning with their ride and long hike through the blizzard, then the bloody fight to get inside the abbey, where it sounded as if the other members of his team were up against determined opposition. Hume had met none, so far, but the monastery creeped him out with all its shadows, nooks and crannies, an abiding sense of dread.

He was entering the dormitory when two figures stepped in front of him, barring his path. One held a garden rake; the other clutched some kind of pointed instrument, held down against his thigh.

Hume faced them squarely, wondering whether he should simply cut them down, then reckoned he should mouth the line O'Connor had dictated to him first.

"We only want the newcomer. Just give us Arthur Watson and—"

The shorter of the two monks tossed his weapon underhand, a silver streak closing the gap between them, slicing through Hume's parka and his jumpsuit, lodging in his gut. He glanced down at the handle of a knife protruding from his torso, astonished at how such a simple thing in untrained hands could finish him.

When he looked up again, the monks were upon him, the rake slashing him with its rusty tines.

As HE REACHED THE other hallway, Bolan heard the clamor of a struggle coming from an open doorway. No gunshots yet, just snarling sounds, as if two animals were grappling for a scrap of food. He moved in that direction, reached the threshold, then eased forward, his Steyr leveled from the waist.

One of the white-clad mercs was going at it with Arthur Watson, hand to hand. They clutched each other in a weird embrace, almost like wrestlers, save for Watson's flailing poker, which he slapped ineffectually against his adversary's back. They were too close and intertwined for Watson to get a decent swing, clutching at the gunman's parka or the hair beneath it with his free hand and twisting, while the shooter hammered Watson's ribs with short, swift blows.

Bolan lifted the Steyr to his shoulder and took aim, but the two combatants spun around, thrashing and cursing, neither of them yet aware they'd acquired an audience. The merc groped for Watson's throat, or maybe he was going for his face, trying to find an eye and gouge it. Watson dropped his chin and bit the hand, sinking his teeth into the web of flesh between the forefinger and thumb.

The shooter howled and whipped a knee toward his opponent's groin, but Watson deflected the blow with a turned-in thigh. Still painful, but not debilitating. Watson impressed Bolan with a head butt to the gunman's face that knocked him backward. He dragged Watson down with him, still leaving no clear-cut target for the Executioner.

Bolan stepped closer, looking for an angle, but the shooter glimpsed him from the corner of his eye as he and Watson fell together. Rolling on the floor, the merc moved swiftly into a seated position behind the accountant, one arm around the man's chest, the other poised below his chin.

Holding a knife.

"You need to lose that piece," he said to Bolan.

"I don't think so."

"Do you wanna watch me cut his throat?"

"It's what you came for," Bolan said. "Me laying down a gun won't stop you."

"Screw that. If you're standing here, it means I've got no backup left. Let's make a deal, eh?"

"We could do that," said Bolan. "Or—"

He put a 5.56 mm bullet through the merc's right eye from ten feet out. The bullet tumbled through his brain and blew out through the back, a bloody halo framed behind the dead man's shattered skull before his arms went slack and he collapsed, leaving Art Watson huddled between his splayed-out legs.

It took a moment, blinking, swiping at the blood that streaked his face, but Watson came around and struggled to his feet unaided, standing up to face his rescuer.

"You saved my life," he said.

"I guess that means you owe me one," Bolan replied.

Watson considered that, frowning, then said, "Depends on what it is."

"Come back and testify," Bolan said. "This is all for nothing, otherwise."

Another silent moment hung between them. Finally, the fugitive accountant spoke up. "No. I mean to stay at Holy Trinity, if they'll still have me."

Movement from the doorway brought Bolan around, his rifle zeroed on another blood-streaked face.

Brother Jerome stood watching them, a cleaver dangling from his right hand.

"There would have to be a vote," the abbot primate said. "But I believe that it can be arranged."

Epilogue

U.S. Global Finance Headquarters, Manhattan

"We warned you, Brad," said Sheldon Page.

Brad Kemper sat ramrod straight before his judges. "So, my people dropped the ball," he said. "There's no denying it. But I can still fix this."

"Fix it?" Cornell Dubois chimed in. "Are you insane?"

"Hardly. Your traitor isn't coming back to testify. I've told you that. Word from the DOJ is that he's standing firm, protected by the church in spite of everything."

"And what about the evidence he carried off?" Reginald Manson was openly scornful. "Is the church protecting that? The copies of our ledgers, canceled checks, computer logs?"

"All circumstantial, if they can't put Watson on the witness stand," said Kemper.

"Christ, you *are* insane," Page sneered at him. "Juries eat up that techno-shit. They'd rather see a spreadsheet than the rat who stole it, any day."

"The evidence could still get lost," said Kemper. "With a man inside—"

"I've heard enough." Page turned to face his partners. "Gentlemen?"

"Enough and then some," Manson said.

"Too much," Dubois agreed.

"You tried your best, Brad," Page allowed. "It simply wasn't good enough. I've told the boys outside to make it qui—"

The *crack* came from behind him, from the giant plate glass window facing Fifth Avenue. Page saw Brad Kemper's head explode and tried to process it, still gaping when there was a second *crack* and Reggie Manson's startled profile burst into a stew of blood and bone chips, scattering across the polished conference table. Manson toppled forward, just as Kemper slithered out of his chair and puddled on the carpet that had cost Page nineteen dollars per square foot.

Sniper! Page thought, trying to rise, stunned to discover that his limbs would not respond to the command. Beside him, to his left, Dubois was faster, springing to his feet, then diving across the table as the third shot tagged him square between his shoulder blades.

Page swiveled to face the shattered window and the high-rise buildings opposite. He couldn't see where Death was coming from, but knew there had to be a fourth shot. Just one more to finish it. He felt a sour laugh or a scream welling inside him as he waited for his life to flash before his eyes.

As BOLAN DISASSEMBLED his Remington 720 sniper rifle, he thought about the monastery and all the monks who had perished. Wiping out U.S. Global wouldn't bring them back to life, but it was the least he could do to serve justice to the men who'd fought bravely by his side, defending their home, their place of worship and their brothers.

He stood at the edge of the rooftop and gazed at the surrounding skyscrapers, the bustling street below. He couldn't say how much evil lurked behind the glass-and-metal facades or in the cars weaving through traffic. The Executioner fought a War Everlasting, and he knew this respite would be brief. What mattered was that he'd done his part to make sure a few more innocent people were safe, and a few more criminals were permanently out of the game.

COMING SOON FROM

GOLD EAGLE

Available December 1, 2015

GOLD EAGLE EXECUTIONER®
FINAL ASSAULT – *Don Pendleton*

When the world's first self-sustaining ship is hijacked and put up for auction, terror groups from around the world are scrambling to make an offer. Mack Bolan must rescue the hostages and destroy the high-tech floating fortress before it's too late.

GOLD EAGLE SUPERBOLAN™
WAR EVERLASTING – *Don Pendleton*

On a desolate ring of islands, Mack Bolan discovers that a reactive volcano isn't the only force about to blow. A Russian mercenary and his group of fanatics are working to destroy America's network of military bases and kill unsuspecting soldiers.

GOLD EAGLE STONY MAN®
EXIT STRATEGY – *Don Pendleton*

One reporter is killed by a black ops group and a second is held captive in Mexico's most dangerous prison. But when Phoenix Force goes in to rescue the journalist, Able Team learns that corruption has infiltrated US law enforcement, threatening both sides of the border.

UPCOMING TITLES FROM

KILL SQUAD
Available March 2016
Nine million dollars goes missing from a Vegas casino, and an accountant threatens to spill to the Feds. But with the mob on his back, the moneyman skips town. Bolan must race across the country to secure the fugitive before the guy's bosses shut him up—forever.

DEATH GAME
Available June 2016
Two American scientists are kidnapped just as North Korea makes a play for Cold War–era ballistic missiles. Determined to save the scientists and prevent a world war, Bolan learns he's not the only one with his sights set on retrieving the missiles...

TERRORIST DISPATCH
Available September 2016
Atrocities continue in the Ukraine and the adjoining Crimean Peninsula, annexed by Russia in March 2014. With no end in sight, a plan is hatched to force American involvement by sending Ukrainian militants to strike Washington, DC, killing civilians and seizing the Lincoln Memorial as protest against their homeland's threat from Russia. Can Bolan bring the war home to the plotters' doorstep?

COMBAT MACHINES
Available December 2016
What began in a Romanian orphanage twenty years earlier, when a man walked away with ten children and disappeared, leads Mack Bolan and a team of Interpol agents to fend off a group of "invisible" assassins carving their way across Europe...toward the USA.

"We need a new plan," he said, looking toward the building where the majority of the fire was coming from.

"The plan is fine," Spence snapped. "It was fine until you had to start making changes. I shouldn't even be here! I'm not a goddamn field agent!"

Bolan didn't waste his breath arguing. Instead, he looked up. The sun was starting to rise. Once they lost the dark, they'd also lose the only real protection they had. The militants would realize they were facing only two men, and they'd swarm them. Bolan and Spence had to take the fight to the enemy.

Bolan popped a smoke canister free from his harness and pulled the pin. He lobbed the grenade over the wall and immediately grabbed for another. "Get ready to move," he said as he sent the second spinning along the narrow street. Colored smoke started spitting into the night air.

"Move where?" Spence demanded.

"Where do you think?" Bolan asked, pointing toward the building. "You said we needed to bring a gift, right? Well, how about we give them the best gift of all—dead enemies."

"Enemy of my enemy is my friend, huh, Cooper?" Spence said in a tone that might have been admiration. He grinned. "I can dig it."

"Then on your feet," Bolan said, freeing a third smoke grenade from his combat harness. He hurled it toward the building as he vaulted over the wall. Smoke flooded the street, caught in the grip of the sea breeze. He and Spence moved forward quickly, firing as they went. They took up positions on either side of the doorway. The smoke was blowing toward them and into the open building. The gunfire had slackened, and Bolan could hear coughing and cursing within.

He caught Spence's attention with a sharp wave. Spence nodded, and Bolan swung back from the door and drove his boot into it. Old hinges, ill-treated by time and the environment, popped loose of the wooden frame with a squeal, and the door toppled inward. Bolan was moving forward even as it fell, his weapon spitting fire. He raked the room beyond, pivoting smoothly, his UMP held at waist height. The gunmen screamed and died.

Bolan stalked forward like Death personified, his gun roaring.

Don't miss
FINAL ASSAULT by Don Pendleton,
available December 2015 wherever
Gold Eagle® books and ebooks are sold.